ALSO BY CONSTANCE LOMBARDO

Mr. Puffball: Stunt Cat to the Stars

HARPER
An Imprint of HarperCollinsPublishers

For my dear sisters,

Amy + Rita

Prologue

The Final Straw Pile

There I stood, atop a huge mound of sticks, stones, crumpled newspapers, and leaves, waiting to die. Or at least be seriously uncomfortable.

For weeks I'd been Director DeMew's stunt cat on a series of educational videos:

This stunt was the worst yet. Fire + toxic smoke + pointy things = big-time ouchies. We'd shot the scene over and over. The fireproof goop applied earlier by Maybelline the makeup cat was wearing thin. Plus my nose itched. How I wished I were elsewhere, sipping a cool glass of lemonade. But I wasn't elsewhere.

I was a stunt cat.

She was a director with a megaphone. "Somebody light that huge mound on fire! Now!"

"Please to wait!" said a voice I knew only too well. My trainer, Bruiser, appeared from out of nowhere and raced over to Director DeMew.

This is the madness, Lady Director! So much of Fire no cat can take! Give Puffyball the breaks!

"CUT!" hissed Director DeMew. "Will somebody tell me why this giant beefcake is in my face?"

One of the crew whispered to Director DeMew (and into her megaphone).

CREW CAT: Bruiser feels we're endangering Mr.
   Puffball with reckless incendiary practices.
DIRECTOR DeMEW: And I should care why?
CREW CAT: Mr. Puffball could get injured.
   Maybe even fatally. Smoke inhalation,
   lacerations, palpitations, etc.
DIRECTOR DeMEW: And I should care why?

This could go on forever. Yes, *Danger* was threaten-
ing to become my middle name, even though I'd prefer
Burt. Or Victor. But I'd signed on the dotted line:

STANDARD STUNT CAT CONTRACT

I, *Mr. Puffball*, hereby waive the right to sue Purramount studios in the event that I suffer, as a result of stunt work: burns, bruises, chafing, loss of fur, lip numbness, toe stubbing, amnesia, hairballs, wardrobe malfunction, frostbite, etc.

Mr. Puffball

YOUR SIGNATURE HERE

So I took a deep breath. "Let's do this thing!"

"Puffyball, you tuff like Bruiser," said Bruiser.

"Mr. Puffball, what really matters," said Maybelline, "is you look great."

Maybelline was right. With my extra-black
bow tie, I looked like a tough-guy celebrity full of
derring-do.

"Quiet on the set!" said Director DeMew. "Take
fifty-two! And . . . action!"

The fire blazed. I blinked against smoke that made
my eyeballs go watery, then dry, and then scorch-
ing. I wriggled free of the ropes and said, "Kids,
don't try this at home."

Then I made my body
hard, squeezed my
eyes shut, and
rolled downhill
through the lick-
ing flames, over
every last poky
bit, to safety at
last.

Two crew cats doused me with cold water. My heart skipped a beat as my flesh went from fiery to freezing in zero seconds flat. I ached all over. "Enough with the ouchy stuff," my brain told my body. "Have you considered law school?"

"Puffy," said Bruiser, slapping me on the back (ow), "you true stunt cat hero guy."

I looked up, way up, into his kind, muscular eyes, and said, "Thanks, Bruiser." But what I thought was, *No. Not anymore.*

I made a wobbly beeline over to Director DeMew to announce my life-changing news, no matter how it might devastate her.

She raised her megaphone and said, "That's a wrap on Cautionary Tails Video #7: *Blazing Fire Mounds and You*!" I shivered before her. "And somebody get this kid a towel."

Time to speak my truth. "Director, being a stunt cat has put me in touch with my manhood. But it's not touching the deepest part of me: my inner movie star. I must follow my bliss. Plus my tail got scorched again. So I've made an important decision: I will stunt no more forever."

6

"But Mr. Puffball, tomorrow we're filming Cautionary Tails Video #8: *Electrical Outlets and Metal Utensils: Friends or Foes?*"

"Sorry, but I'm through. And no amount of cajoling, begging, or offers of huge sums of cash—" Before I could finish my sentence, Director DeMew raised her megaphone once more.

SOMEBODY GET ME A NEW STUNT CAT!!!!

And so ended my days of being Mr. Puffball, Stunt Cat to the Stars Or did it?

My Journey Thus Far

Let me take you back to the days when a New Jersey kitten dreamed of something more. Something more glamorous. Something more bright lights and limos. Something more sequins, paparazzi, and bow ties.

That kitten, who was me, Mr. Puffball, left his ancestral home and traveled clear across the map to become a famous Hollywood movie star. Along the way he narrowly escaped tornadoes, aliens, condors, and hobo initiation by the hobos of Hobowood.

When he finally reached Hollywood, he got a Feline Divine makeover by Ms. Lola and was united with his signature bow tie. He strode over to an MGM audition only to find he'd missed it. Then he discovered something better than stardom—the kind of legendary cats you read about, like you're doing right here:

CHESTER P. GRUMPUS III A.K.A CHET

Famed director of *The Karate Kit*, *Titanicat*, and *Night at the Meowseum*

WHISKERS

Dancer extraordinaire!

KITTY LaRUE

Charming chanteuse

ROSIE

Adorable best friend!

BRUISER

Stunt cat trainer to the stars!

EL GATO

Mega-movie star and former frenemy. Currently: friend

With their help, I was transformed from meh to fabulous:

And now El Gato has asked me to costar in his upcoming buddy movie. That he's starring in! With the excellent working title *Mac & Cheesy's Excellent Adventure.*

Costar! With El Gato! Me! I know!!

Have you ever seen a buddy movie? They look something like this:

This would be my "star vehicle," as we call it in the biz. A star vehicle is a blockbuster movie that transforms an ordinary cat (moi) into a superstar (future moi!).

QUESTION: Was the buddy movie a go?
ANSWER: Kinda.
QUESTION: What does *kinda* mean?
ANSWER: Kinda means kind of. Yes, we had the concept: a buddy movie. Yes, we had the stars: El Gato and me. And yes, we had a script by professional writers.

The only missing piece was *Lights! Camera! Action!* Which should happen very soon.

Or so I thought, until El Gato came over one day to deliver a sizable bump in my road to stardom. "Ready to start filming, buddy?" I asked, plopping down a bowl of his favorite yogurt-covered mouse tails.

"Mmmglbbhaebglub . . ."

"Chew, swallow, talk."

Gulp. "Almost. We have one more thing to do: meet the suits. I hope they haven't seen this lousy review."

"Don't listen to the naysayers," I said. "You look great."

"I'm going to look great," said El Gato, "because I'm on a special celebrity diet. The same one Mewly Cyrus is on."

"What's the diet?"

"I can eat anything I want, except kale."

"You never eat kale anyway."

"That's why this diet's perfect for me." He spilled a boxful of cheese crackers into his mouth. "So I'll see you tomorrow morning at Purramount Studios. And we'll talk to those suits. We'll iron everything out with the suits. We won't let them get rumpled."

"Excellent."

What was El Gato talking about? I didn't know. I had never ironed or rumpled a suit in my life. But I wasn't about to let my ignorance show. Whoever these suits were, I would meet them head on.

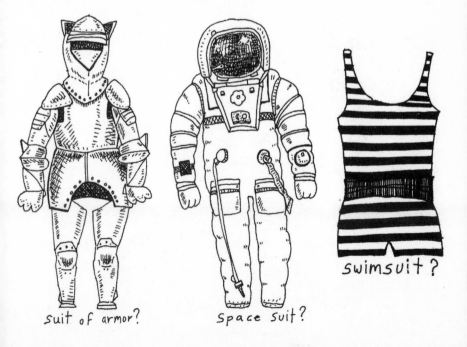

suit of armor?   space suit?   swimsuit?

Meet the Suits

Turns out *suits* is another word for head honchos, big kahunas, top cats, etc. Meaning El Gato and I were meeting the Purramount Studios executives to beg them for money to pay for:

Director / DeMew.

costumes!

Film equipment!

Professional snakes!

EXTRAS!

Just thinking about it made my wallet hurt. It would take all of El Gato's star power plus all of my natural charm to convince those suits to give us the hundreds and hundreds of dollars needed to make our buddy movie.

The morning of the meeting, I opened the front door and found myself face-to-face with a cat I'd never seen before.

"Mr. Puffball?" I nodded. "I have a message from El Gato."

"Are you going to deliver it via singing telegram?" I asked hopefully.

"No, I'm going to tell you to look up."

I looked up:

Too much catnip - Must stay in bed - go meet suits alone - Knock 'em dead!

Meet the suits alone? No! Not! No way!

How would El Gato's star power and my irresistible charm convince the Purramount executives to fund our buddy movie, *Mac & Cheesy's Excellent Adventure,* if El Gato wasn't there?

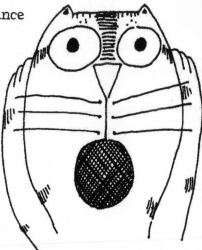

I needed a way to make sure El Gato would be at the meeting even though he was home in bed.

I rushed to my planning basket and brainstormed ideas.

* Bring along a hologram of El Gato?
  Too science-y!
* A lifelike cardboard cutout?
  Too cardboard-y!
* Record El Gato comments in his voice and tell the suits, "He's hiding in my backpack because he's self-conscious about his weight?"
  Too weight-y!

I thought and I thought. And then I thought of the movie *Kitty Doubtfire.* See where I'm going here? That scene in the restaurant where the tomcat has to be both himself and Kitty Doubtfire?

Aha moment! Here was the plan:

Step one: Stuff an El Gato costume into my backpack.

Step two: Whistle my way over to Purramount Studios.

Step three: Sneak past the receptionist.

Then it was time to act like I'd never acted before!
I found a door bearing the mark of the suits:

Inside were the executives who could make our buddy movie a reality.

I reached for the handle, dressed in a classic black bow tie from my personal collection. First the suits would meet the talented Mr. Puffball.

The door swung open. One suit looked up and said, "Who let this guy into the Room of Important Cats?" I glared at him with eyes that said "Rude." Then I looked over my shoulder as if talking to somebody in the hallway. "What's that, El Gato? You need to use the litter box? No problemo."

I lowered myself into an overstuffed seat. "Greetings, Purramount executives, I'm Mr. Puffball, former stunt cat to the stars and the Unimportant Sheriff in *Nine Lives to Live*. In case you didn't hear, El Gato had to go." I chuckled and rolled my eyes. "He goes a lot. He'll be back soon, though." I flashed my winningest smile.

No response. Nothing. Nada.

Awkward!

Just then, a tall she-cat walked in and sat down. "I'm Victoria Bossypaws, commander in chief of Purramount Studios. And you're Mr. Puffball, correct? Where's El Gato?"

"He's finishing up in the litter box. But he'll be back soon."

"Well," said Ms. Bossypaws, "I have good news, and I have bad news. The good news: We want to make your movie, *Mac & Cheesy's Excellent Adventure . . .*"

I jumped onto the table and whooped!

"Wait until El Gato hears this! I'll go get him." I ran out, ducked into an empty room, changed into El Gato's costume, and returned to the Room of Important Cats.

"Greetings, Ms. Bossypaws! My colleague and BFF Mr. Puffball tells me you have delightful news to share!"

El Gato, please explain why your whiskers look exactly like Mr. Puffball's.

"Good noticing, Ms. Bossypaws!" I said in my best El Gato voice. "It's going to be great working together!"

Victoria Bossypaws put on her irritated eyebrows. "Mr. Puffball didn't wait for the bad news. We do want to make the movie—"

"That's good news!"

"—BUT you won't be in it. We found other actors who bring youthful energy and international flavor . . ."

"That is bad news!" I jumped up again. I needed time to think. And cry. "Sorry, everyone. I have to

22

go again. Blame my jumbo breakfast smoothie!" I ran from the room, ripped off the costume, let out a quiet sob, and hurried back.

"El Gato was babbling nonsense," I said, pointing toward the hall. "You want other actors to do our buddy movie?!"

"Correct. We found the perfect dynamic duo," said Ms. Bossypaws. "Dim the lights!"

"Cumbercat and Claw?" I said.

"*Hiss!* El Gato will be furious when he gets up . . . I mean, gets back."

"Where is El Gato?" said one suit.

"Maybe he's at the snack bar," said another.

I covered my mouth and threw my voice into a distant yowl. "I hear him yowling in the hall. I better get him!" I ran out and reappeared as El Gato.

"Is this because Benedict's so slender?" I asked (as El Gato). "Is it his irresistible British accent? Because I can fake an accent, too. Jolly good. Tallyho— Or I can do French. Zis is not a croissant! Australian: G'day, mate. Have you seen my dingo?"

Victoria Bossypaws slammed the table, and the room quieted. "Somebody turn on the lights! This is bigger than accents. El Gato is the past. We're Purramount Studios, and we're the future. And so is Benedict Cumbercat. Here's the scientific proof."

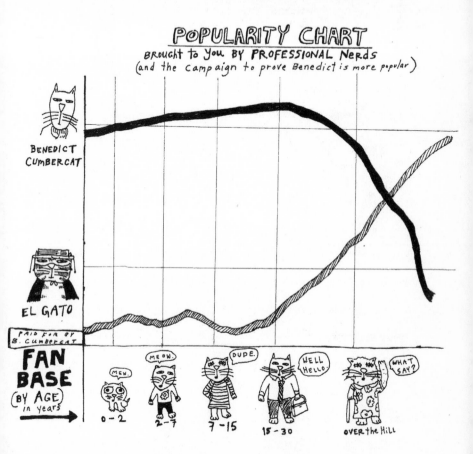

POPULARITY CHART
BROUGHT to YOU BY PROFESSIONAL NeRdS
(and the campaign to prove Benedict is more popular)

BENEDICT CUMBERCAT

EL GATO

PAID FOR BY B. CUMBERCAT

FAN BASE (BY AGE) in years →

MEW — 0 - 2
MEOW — 2 - 7
DUDE. — 7 - 15
WELL HELLO — 15 - 30
WHAT SAY? — OVER the HiLL

One of my paws wanted to bang the table in utter despair. My other paw wanted to punch this tidal wave of totally unfair.

Either way, it was time to do something big.

Star Vehicle

"If Benedict Cumbercat is so awesome," I said, still dressed as El Gato, "can he do this?"

"Or tap dance like Mr. Puffball? I'll get him now."

I left quickly and returned as my buddy, Mr. Puffball. Meaning myself. It was getting confusing.

"Why are you wearing El Gato's hat?" asked Victoria Bossypaws with a suspiciously raised eyebrow.

"Funny you should ask . . ."

Just then the door burst open. Guess who had woken up and decided to come to the meeting after all?

"I made it!" cried El Gato. "Why are you wearing my hat?"

"Hey ho, buddy! Isn't it terrible how Benedict Cumbercat and Jude Claw are trying to steal our buddy movie?"

"I KNOW! Even though you already knew, because you've been here all along, it's still shocking."

27

Ms. Bossypaws slammed the table again. "We've already been through this! Benedict and Jude Claw hand-delivered an impressive demo reel, in which they do buddy-movie-like things at famous landmarks all over California."

"But we already paid the monkeys to write our script," said El Gato.

"Paid them how? In bananas from the Purramount cafeteria?" Ms. Bossypaws asked, whiskers twitching. "Our decision is final! Benedict Cumbercat will be the star of *Mac & Cheesy's Excellent Adventure*!"

"No way!" shouted El Gato. (I knew he'd save the day.) "Not as long as I have something Cumbercat will never have."

"What's that?" asked Ms. Bossypaws.

"A one hundred percent Corinthian leather cape. And a hat with movie star pom-poms."

Now Ms. Bossypaws' angry eyebrows were in full swing. I had to think fast.

Picture this, Ms. Bossypaws: EL Gato + I will make a better demo reel. A bigger demo reel. Because we are the FUTURE!

"What sort of demo reel?" she asked.

El Gato and I looked at each other and said, "The sort of demo reel where . . ."

"We go to Las Vegas! With the bright lights. And replicas!"

"And . . . ?" said Ms. Bossypaws.

"We go to diners," said El Gato. "With revolving dessert cases."

Ms. Bossypaws crossed her paws over her chest. "And . . . ?"

"And say hysterical things that make kittens laugh so hard milk squirts out their noses. Like . . ."

"Pie?"

"That's right," I said, glancing at El Gato, but his eyes had turned to pies.

"And?" said Ms. Bossypaws.

I think it was the word *pie* that sent El Gato into a trance where he could only utter food words. I had to improvise around the madness.

"Eggs Benedict," he murmured.

"Is Benedict going to do this movie? No way!"

"Casserole."

"Cats a roll all the way to the Grand Canyon!"

"Hoagie?"

"Hokeydokey!" I said. "Do you love it, Ms. Bossypaws?"

"Love is a strong word," she said.

"Imagine, if you will: El Gato and me, goin' on a grand trip."

"Coney Island clam strip?" asked El Gato.

Now he'd gone too far. Coney Island is in Brooklyn. New York. All the way on the other side of the map. We didn't have time for Coney Island.

"If you can film all that," said Ms. Bossypaws, "including Coney Island, and get that demo reel into my paws in two weeks, you just might be the stars of *Mac & Cheesy's Excellent Adventure.*"

El Gato snapped out of his trance. But his mind was still on the menu. "How will we get to all that food when my ice machine exploded and destroyed my limo?"

"We're movie stars. We'll fly!"

"No way. Remember what
happened last time I
flew?"

"Well then, we'll
just have to take . . ."

"Yes?" hissed Victoria Bossypaws.

Think, Mr. Puffball! I didn't own a car, a scooter, or
even a go-kart. But I needed to get us from Hollywood,
California, to Coney Island, New York, and back again
in two weeks. So I blurted the first thing that popped
into my head. "We'll use . . . the star vehicle!"

And then I sighed a big, big sigh. My brilliant
plan was doomed before it had even begun. Because
there was no star vehicle.

Or was there?

Directions

"How did you know about the star vehicle?" asked El Gato as we trudged back to MGM Studios.

"I made it up."

"Strange. One of my admirers gave me this."

"Wow." The fates were clearly on our side. And yet, I had to stop and scratch my head. Not because I had fleas (which I don't!).

"Do we know how to make a high-quality short demo reel?" I asked El Gato.

"I've been in tons of movies. How hard could it be?"

Phew! "Then let's brainstorm ideas to make this the best demo reel ever."

"If Victoria Bossypaws wants the future, how about a time machine? Time machines are all about the future, unless you travel into the past."

"Where in the world are we going to get a time machine?" I asked.

"I don't like your cat-titude," said El Gato.

"Let's go to the screening room," I said, once we reached MGM Studios. "It's the perfect place for brainstorming. There's a chalkboard."

But outside the screening room, we were stopped by this sign:

You, too, Can Be A
Great Director!
INSTRUCTOR: (BUT YOU can call him Chet.)
Chester P. Grumpus III
Testing in session
shhhhhhhh!
→ sign handmade by Whiskers... with love!

El Gato and I peeked into the little window.

"Pretend this is an actor," Chet was saying to Rosie, while wrapping a scarf around a potted fern. "Now tell me what this scene's about."

"Um . . . this scene's about a kung fu cat who must save the world from the evil Dr. Woof. And . . . action!"

"Good use of the word *action*," said Chet. "But first, how will you get to the emotional heart of the scene? Talk to your actor. You can call her . . . Fern. Use the megaphone!"

"What do you say to the camera-cats?" asked Chet.

Rosie turned to a row of chairs and said, "Zoom in, cats!"

"What else, dang it?!" yelled Chet. I'd never seen him so animated.

"Turn up the microphones! More props! FOCUS!"

Just then the door swung open, and I fell sprawling into the room.

"Simmer down, kid," said Chet. "We're about to screen Rosie's final project: a two-and-a-half-minute movie based on the first known movie with live recorded sound."

Kitty came in with a big bowl of popcorn, and Whiskers mamboed in behind her, turning off the lights.

"Good job, Rosie!" I said as everybody applauded.

"She's a fast learner," said Chet. "But there's a lot to learn. Now, what happened this morning with the suits?"

"Benedict Cumbercat's trying to steal our movie. . . ."

"That explains this," said Rosie.

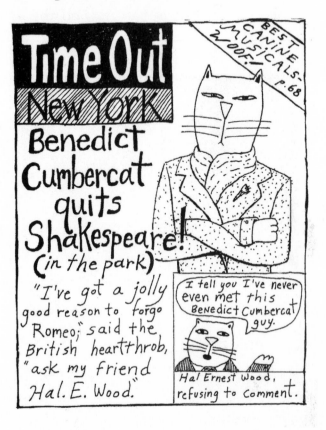

"Benedict does have a cute accent," said Kitty.

"Even so," I said, "because of him, we have to make an extremely impressive demo reel at landmarks across America."

"I wish we could help you kids," said Chet, "but we're off to Chicago to shoot *Bonnie and Clawed*."

"Starring who?" El Gato and I both yelled.

"I thought of asking you two," said Chet. "But Bonnie is a she-cat. So I asked Jennifer Pawprints. And Benedict Cumbercat. They'll be adorable together."

"I could be a she-cat," said El Gato.

"El Gato and I are adorable together," I said.

Chet shook his head. "Sorry, Mr. Puffball, but you don't have an English accent."

"Since when is being English *SO SPECIAL?*" shouted El Gato.

"Okay, El Gato," said Rosie in a calm voice, "time to assume the pose. Everybody join in."

"Now back to business. What you really need for your demo reel is a director; somebody to handle the lighting, cinematic style, dialogue, and budget. While staying on schedule."

"Who in the world could do all that?" I said.

Rosie raised her megaphone. "You're looking at her."

I nudged Rosie out of the way. "I don't see anybody."

"Rosie means she can do it," said Kitty.

"Absolutely," said Chet. "And this certificate proves it."

Chet University

UPON COMPLETION OF THE COURSE

You too can be a . . .

Great Director

Chester P. Grumpus III (but you can call him Chet) hereby confers upon

Rosie Pringle

having demonstrated abilities in directorship

Magna Cat Laude, may now try her paw at directing a movie for real.

YES SHE CAN!

Chester Percival Grumpus III
DEAN OF THE "UNIVERSITY"

Whiskers
DIPLOMA DESIGNER

"Perfect! Can you also drive the star vehicle? It's waiting for us at the Purramount Studios garage."

"I'll be too busy developing scenes and scouting locations from the passenger seat. But I know the perfect driver. Let's all meet at the garage tomorrow morning. I promise he'll be there."

"Yeah, baby!" I said, like I do when I get excited. "We'll have a Cross-Country Road Trip Demo Reel Adventure in the star vehicle with our mystery driver! Chet, is it okay if we stop by the set in Chicago? I'd like to meet my rival."

"Do it and I'll put you in a scene." He held out his paw. "No hard feelings?"

"Of course not," I said, shaking his paw. Benedict Cumbercat was a great actor. He could star in every comedy, mystery, and monster movie Hollywood made for the next hundred years. But he wasn't going to star in my buddy movie.

Rosie, El Gato, the mystery driver, and I were now a kick-butt team! We'd film an awesome demo reel across America and return in two weeks to steal back our buddy movie. We made a list of all we needed for our Cross-Country Road Trip Demo Reel Adventure and called it:

ALL WE NEED FOR OUR CROSS-COUNTRY ROAD TRIP DEMO REEL ADVENTURE

1. Water (some of America is desert)
2. Nighty-night necessities (sleeping bags, blankies, pillows, sleeping masks)
3. Film equipment (cameras, mics, sound-effect machine, director's chair, and beret)

4. Flares, in case we need more flare
5. A variety of maps, from every place in the forty-eight contiguous states (whatever that means!)
6. Dried sardines, mouse jerky, hard candy, chewing gum, cheesy crackers, pretzels, peanut butter, and a bit of catnip for late-night driving

"And to help get us in the mood," said Rosie, "there's a buddy movie marathon tonight at the local drive-in."

"What are we waiting for?"

In the Driver's Seat

"Put these on," said Rosie, handing me clothes when I arrived at the studio garage the next day. I did as directed. After all, Rosie's the director!

I feel like that guy from MAD MANX: FURRY ROAD.

"What's up with the crazy outfit?" asked El Gato.

"And when is the driver arriving?" I asked.

"You'll see," she said mysteriously.

Inside the garage was an amazing collection of famous movie vehicles.

The Star Trek *Enterprise*

The Back to the Future DeLorean

Gromit's airplane from
The Curse of the Were-Rabbit

The Ghostbusters
Cadillac

El Gato led us to our ride.

"Sweet wheels," said Rosie.

"I like the rest of the van, too," I said. "But where's the mystery driver?"

"Surprise!"

"Where?"

"The mystery driver," said Rosie, "is the cat who, for the last year, has begged me for driving lessons. He's the cat who is dressed like a driver. And he's standing exactly where you're standing, Mr. Puffball."

"Where?" I asked, spinning in a circle.

"She means you," said El Gato, climbing inside.

Where's the mini-FRIDGE? AND COMFY PILLOWS? AND SALMON AIR FRESHENER? I'M HUNGRY!!!

"Assume the position, El Gato," said Rosie in a calm voice.

El Gato pressed his palms together. "Calmness is me. I suppose."

"Now let's start our Cross-Country Road Trip Demo Reel Adventure!" said Rosie, opening the passenger door.

"Thanks, Rosie," I said, heading in before being yanked back by my scarf.

"The driver gets into the driver's seat," she said.

"So soon?"

"Just get in."

I hoisted myself into the driver's seat, banging my head against the steering wheel only twice.

"Try and buckle up without hurting yourself, Mr. Puffball."

I grasped the steering wheel with sweaty paws. Yes, I'd been a stunt cat who toppled into unbelievably deep chasms. Yes, I'd been set on fire. Yes, quicksand. But driving?!

Rosie shoved the key at me, and I stuck it in the keyhole like an ace and rotated the wheel thingy like a pro.

"Let's get revved!" I made authentic vrooming noises and one accidental honking noise from the rear. Driving was easier than I thought!

"Mr. Puffball!"

"What?" I asked, slamming on the brake. "Am I about to hit a squirrel?"

"How can you hit a squirrel when you're not moving? Now turn the key, put the gear into D for drive, and gently step on the gas."

I did as instructed, and we rolled smoothly out of the garage.

"Stop!" said Rosie.

Screech! "Squirrel again?"

Somebody was banging on my window.

"I'll try to make you proud," said Rosie.

"Just remember, when you hold up that megaphone, you hold up a century-long tradition." He turned and walked away, waving his cane, yelling, "Directors rule!"

"Being the director is a big deal," I said.

"But actors rule," said El Gato irritably.

"Calmness is you," said Rosie.

"I hope you know how to read that map," I said to Rosie, who had a big one unfolded on her lap.

"Do you think she-cats can't read maps, Mr. Puffball?"

"Well, toms do have a more natural sense of direction."

"Is that why you just missed our exit?"

"What's an exit?"

Las Vegas, Nevada, was our first stop. Because what says "buddy movie" more than a wild and crazy night in Vegas?

"Here it is!" said Rosie, pointing to a spot on the map.

"That's only two inches away!" I said.

"Two inches on the map equals two hundred and seventy-five miles," she said. "Now, eyes on the road! Easy on the gas pedal! Paws on the steering wheel! Las Vegas, here we come."

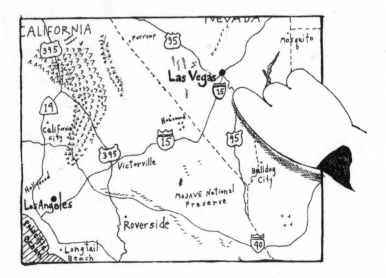

Just then some colorful billboards came into view.
"And stop staring at billboards," added Rosie.

"You're doing great, Mr. Puffball," Rosie said. "And heading in the right direction. I'm going to play this CD so I can take a cat nap."

Then I drove for hours, while learning lots of driver lingo from the CD:

- **East & west:** In the west, east is away from the coast. In the east, west is away from the coast. Try making sense of that!
- **North & south:** North goes to Canada. If you keep going north, bring warm clothes!! South goes to Mexico. If you keep going south, bring a bathing suit!
- **AM & FM:** These are totally different radio places.
- **Windshield wipers:** Press a button and liquid

cleaner sprays out, followed by windshield wiper action. Yes, it's as fun as it sounds. Don't press too often, or it will stop working.

- **Your paws:** Must be on the driving wheel thingy at all times or your van goes berserk.
- **Gas pedal vs. brake pedal:** Gas = go. Brake = stop. Choose one. Not both! Or scary noises happen.

I listened to the CD over and over, but still we weren't in Las Vegas.

"Does the map think I'm still going the right way?" I asked Rosie.

The only response was "Zzzzz." It was even louder from the backseat, where El Gato was holding his own snoring marathon.

I was driving solo! *You saw that spot on the map clear as day*, I told myself. *All you have to do is stay on this road until you find it.*

By the time I saw the sign through the darkness, I was half asleep. So I veered off the road and stepped on the brake, à la the CD instructions in the section "Brake Equals Stop." The jarring jump and lunge of the van as I screeched to a stop wasn't loud enough to wake my passengers (success!). I put it on *P* for park (à la "Gear Changes and You!"), crawled into the back of the van, slipped into my sleeping bag, and snuggled in.

As I drifted toward dreamland, my mind swirled! I, Mr. Puffball, was on the road with my two favorite cats, heading across the country, having wild adventures, and learning to drive. The next morning, we'd start filming our demo reel to beat all demo reels.

What could possibly go wrong?

Hobo Crossing

*I*t was like a nightmare become reality.

First my ears were blasted by the scraping sound of metal doors. Next a million paws dragged me across the van floor. *Bumpety-bump-bump* bumped my head along the hard surface. Then I was yanked out into the harsh reality of morning, blinking against the sunlight, until finally my eyes adjusted and:

"What are you guys doing in Las Vegas?"

The hobos shook their heads. "This ain't no Vegas!"

"What about the sign I saw last night?"

The doors of the van sprung open, and out popped Rosie, followed by El Gato.

The hobos laughed. "Your friend sure is . . ." I pulled off his sleeping mask. "*Gasp!* Is that El Gato?"

"El Gato is a Monday Night at the Movies favorite!" said one hobo.

58

"We voted him Cat Most Likely to Be in a Movie We Like!" said another.

"Perfect timing," said a third. "You folks are about to meet another Hollywood friend!"

They tramped off toward the train tracks, and we followed.

"Whoo-whoo!" A loud whistle blew. Suddenly a huge cat jumped out of an open car.

Bruiser!

He landed on his paws after a perfect flip and said, "Mr. Puffyball! How you here?"

"Driving lesson mishap. What about you?"

"Let's go Hobowood for Bruiser explaining." Soon we were there, sitting on logs, holding tin cups of milk, and listening to:

THE TALE OF BRUISER

"The country of my kittenhood was too poor for trains, but one in our village talked of America, with trains in every place. His stories got into my brain like a brain worm, which were plenty in my country and another reason for leave. But who can cross tundra? I Bruiser. I strong like bull. I cross rock mountains and ice fields until I reach big water. I swim. One day shark come for bite my tail, but I show muscles and say, 'I maybe punch you hard in nose.' He take me to America in exchange for not punching. I ride shark happy through cold water and sing song of my village, 'Oh, the rocks we eat they make us strong . . .'"

Bruiser sang like a mastiff with the flu. It had to stop. "What happened next, Bruiser?"

"We land in the California. Shark give me tooth for remember him." Bruiser pulled his collar down to show us a shark-tooth necklace. "Soon I see the iron giant speeding to me, and I know what is. Train. I grab rocks, eat for strength, run fast like bull and jump into." He snapped his fingers, which most cats cannot do.

"And landed right in our car," said one of the hobos. "Scared the stripes clean off me."

"This is yes," said Bruiser. "American cats small. Scared. But I smile, make nice, they give beans, invite me for be strong cat hobo. I love trains, so, sure, yes. The end."

"But Bruiser," I asked, "how'd you end up in Hollywood training stunt cats?"

"One day Director DeMew visit Hobowood. She make documentary for new celebrity diet called 'eating beans only.' She ask, 'Who you?' I know little English then and say, 'Train!' She say, 'Well then, come Hollywood. Train stunt cats.' I don't know what means. But I do. Then she ask, 'What is name?' I write and show her. Like this."

She say, "We call you Bruiser. The end."

"What've you been up to in Hollywood, Mr. Puff-ball?" asked a hobo.

I stuck out my chest. "Ever heard of the movie *Nine Lives to Live?*"

"Heard of it? Why, we spent our last nickel to see it in the theater."

"Yeah," said another hobo. "I sure wish we'd kept that nickel jar. We're low on beans again."

The dinner bell rang. Soon we were all slurping up beans while I told entertaining tales about Hollywood.

After dinner, the hobos said, "Time for a genuine hobo show! Hollywood folk, join in!"

Rosie set up the camera as the hobos rushed the makeshift stage. Two plucked banjos. Bruiser juggled three rocks, two logs, and a volunteer squirrel. Several did interpretive dance using scarves and tambourines. Stage left, a lone hobo broke into mime.

"In this scene," Rosie said, "the hobos will . . ." But there was no scene. The hobos weren't even listening. Rosie put on her angry director eyebrows and raised her megaphone. "CUT!! Did I say *action*? Who has the script?"

The hobos were now forming a hobo pyramid. I had to step in and quick. "Maybe the hobo show is background for a hilarious exchange between me and El Gato," I said. "I'll dare him to eat many, many beans. We can splice in the beans later."

"Let's have a big build-up using dialogue," she said, turning the camera on El Gato and me. "And . . . action!"

Rosie raised her megaphone. "CUT! I forgot to take off the lens cap. Let's try that again. Bean Challenge Scene, take two!"

"Looks like the lens cap is still on," I said, reaching toward the camera.

"No." She screwed it on. "Now it's on." She unscrewed it. "Now it's off. On. Off. See the difference?"

"Got it. Ready to start filming again?"

But suddenly . . .

"Somebody's in the canteen after hours!" yelled one of the hobos. We rushed over, and here's what we found:

"El Gato ate beans after bean-eating time," said a hobo.

"He's violated the Hobo Code of Honor!"

"I don't care if he is a celebrity. Nobody raids our bean stash! Let's get 'em!"

Faster than you can say Beano, El Gato jumped up and ducked, rolled, and wove through the crowd until he was racing out the door.

Rosie and I were right behind him. "Maybe you

should put down the camera!" I said as the horde of angry hobos closed in.

"No way!" she yelled. "This is gold!"

We lost them for a second and dove behind some bushes. I grabbed El Gato's outfit right off him. "Get the van and meet me behind the canteen."

Suddenly Bruiser was next to me. "How I help, Puffyball?"

"Have you got a trampoline?"

"Of course, yes."

"Bring it to the canteen!"

Bruiser veered off. The van started up, and I swerved toward the canteen, just ahead of the hobos. Bruiser held out the trampoline. "Thanks, Bruiser!" I leapt onto it, catapulted to the roof of the canteen, and ran toward the back. The van was almost there, and the back doors were open. "Don't stop!"

"You'll never make it, Mr. Puffball!" yelled Rosie, driving and filming at the same time.

"Yes, I will. I'm a stunt cat!" And so I dove, using the cape as a gliding device, the crowd muttering angrily below. And *wham!*—I was in.

"That's a wrap!" said Rosie. El Gato was already asleep.

As we sped away, I pulled off El Gato's costume, turned toward the hobos, and waved. "Still friends?"

The hobos were good cats. I knew they'd forgive me. After all, the Hobo Code of Honor includes not holding a grudge for more than forty-eight hours.

BAM! Something landed on the roof. Now he was climbing inside—

"Bruiser! Did the hobos throw you out?"

"No. I think Puffyball need Bruiser helps. I read *Variety*. I know of demo reel, yes? Okay I come with?"

If we had this much trouble with a group of friendly hobos, what would happen when we went out into the real America, with its bears and dogs and sports enthusiasts? Having a burly buddy along could be just the ticket.

"Sure, Bruiser!"

Viva Las Vegas

"**P**lease to roll down windows now!"

Bruiser was right. Why should we suffer through the malodorous side effects of El Gato's bean spree? Was it my fault El Gato didn't understand the language of winking?

We crossed the California state line into Nevada with moi at the wheel.

"We need to plan out this demo reel," said Rosie. "Let's lay it out scene by scene, destination by destination, so we don't have a repeat of the hobo fiasco."

All the awake cats brainstormed a plan for our demo reel at landmarks across America and called it:

A PLAN FOR OUR DEMO REEL AT LANDMARKS ACROSS AMERICA

● **Las Vegas**—"Oooh," said Rosie, bouncing in her seat. "Las Vegas has a small replica of the Brooklyn Bridge. Close up on Mr. Puffball and El Gato strolling over it. Pan out to reveal they're actually in Las Vegas. Mr. Puffball says, 'I didn't know the Brooklyn Bridge stretched all the way to Nevada!'"

● **Grand Canyon**—"Through clever editing," Rosie explained, "I'll make it look like you're leaping over the Grand Canyon. Mr. Puffball, you'll say, 'Aaaaaaaah!! It's hard to believe we're jumping over the Grand Canyon!' And El Gato will say, 'But, aaaaaahhhh, we really are!!'"

- **The Wild West**—"Even though it's no longer wild and not even that far west," I said, "I hear there are ghost towns and rodeos all over." "Perfect!" squealed Rosie. "You two can put on ten-gallon hats, and I'll ask a horse to help us stage a wild and crazy rodeo scene!"

- **Mount Rushmore**—You know those ginormous presidential heads carved into the mountain looking all presidential? One of the great chase scenes in cinematic history was filmed there by Alfred Hitchcat himself in the movie *North by Northwest*.

"This great art of America we must respect," said Bruiser. "So I put El Gato into."

"WHAT?"

"I chisel you too, Puffyball. To help career."

"Bruiser!" said Rosie. But he was lost in thought.

"BRUISER!" That got his attention. She put down the megaphone. "It's time to ask ourselves: WWCD?"

"Meaning what?" I asked.

"Meaning: What would Chet do?"

"Play checkers?" I guessed.

"AND," said Rosie, "he'd stay on schedule. Our schedule does not include time for carving huge faces into mountainsides."

"This is the pity," said Bruiser.

"Rosie's got a point," I said. But just then our favorite song came on the radio, and we had to sing along.

The song ended, so I switched off the radio so we could keep singing.

"What does the wolf say?" I sang.

"Howl, howl, howl, howl, howl, howling!" answered Rosie and Bruiser.

"And what does the cow say?"

"Moo, moo, moo, moo, moo, moo, moo!"

"And what does the sloth say?"

Silence. I had to think of a more vocal animal.

"What does the fish say?"

Silence again. I thought harder.

"And what does the alligator say?"

"Zzzzzzzzz."

"No, he does not say zzzz . . ." I turned my head. *Oh.* They'd fallen asleep.

Time to drive solo again. This time, no mistakes. I took the correct exit for Las Vegas and drove until I saw a parking lot. Parking in a designated parking lot was easy. I was becoming a real driving ace!

I catnapped until the Nevada sun streamed through our windshield. Something less pleasant was also at our windshield.

El Gato woke up and started screaming, which jolted Rosie and Bruiser awake, and sent the tiny dinosaur scurrying. We stretched and spilled out into the streets of fabulous Las Vegas, the perfect setting for our first successful scene.

"This is your director," megaphoned Rosie, "directing you toward the mini Brooklyn Bridge."

El Gato cupped his paws to make his own megaphone. "And this is your celebrity! Insisting that our first scene be at the Hard Rock Cafe, where we'll stuff our faces full of crab cakes."

(*Note to the reader:* We did stuff our faces with

crab cakes. Think a mountain of crab cakes quickly reduced to one left on the plate, El Gato and me eyeballing it, paws shooting out simultaneously, crab-cake fight, etc. It got ugly. Real ugly.)

"Here is sure the best idea," said Bruiser, pointing across the street after we'd left the Hard Rock Cafe:

CIRQUE DU SOLEIL
PRESENTS
Merrie Olde England

"This crazy circus place where talent cats to balance on higher wires. And acrobatics fly through air with greatest of easy. And sequins like even Hollywood types never seen. In another word, best place everywhere!"

"Sounds great," said El Gato, squinting at the marquee. "Except . . . *oh no!*"

TONIGHT'S CELEBRITY:
Benedict Cumbercat

"That cat's everywhere," I said.

"Let's go inside and show them a real celebrity," said El Gato.

"Hey," said the ticket tabby. "Aren't you the world-famous El Gato?"

"He is," I said. "And I'm the fantastic Mr. Puffball, and this is the valiant Bruiser and the multitalented Rosie. And we'd all like to go inside, please."

"You and every other cat in Vegas, which is why we're completely sold out."

"But this is El Gato!" I said.

"And these are how many tickets I can sell him."

Suddenly someone came storming out of the theater.

I'm too good for the circus! Find another celebrity! And I'm not returning this outfit either.

It was Benedict Cumbercat in the fur. He was tall. He was handsome. He had that indescribable quality I can only describe as indescribable.

He glanced at El Gato, and a sly smile crossed his face. And then—*zip!*—he was gone, never to be seen again for a bit.

"Was that who I think it was?" said El Gato.

"I think it was."

One second later, another cat tore out of the theater. He was wearing a name tag that read *Gustave—General Manager*, and his tail was whipping around in a panic. "The show's about to start! Where can I find a replacement celebrity at this late hour?" He looked our way, and his eyes lit up. "El Gato! Marvelous! You're just the cat Gustave needs!"

"Do you also need El Gato's stunt cat?" Then I whispered to the gang, "Looks like we've struck buddy movie demo reel gold!"

"And a kung fu cat?" asked Rosie.

"And too you are wanting me?"

"Bruiser!" said Gustave.

I looked at Bruiser with questioning eyebrows. "Bruiser work much places in America."

"Gustave can use all you marvelous cats. Follow me."

And off we went to our next fun adventure, one that would prove we weren't:

1. rushing into things we didn't understand,
2. getting into tons of trouble, and
3. generally ruining everything we touched.

Not!

Cirque du Soleil

We went inside, following Gustave through a maze of hallways and past a parade of exotic cats:

To each one, Gustave said, "Dahling, you look marvelous." Then he pulled us into a room with a glittery gold star on the door.

"Here's the deal," said Gustave. "It's Merrie Olde England night at Cirque du Soleil. We'll have music by the Beetles, of course. A firework display of the British flag and a giant cup of tea. And we were supposed to have Benedict Cumbercat reciting that famous Shakespearean monologue from *Hamlet*."

"You mean: 'To mew or not to mew, that is the question'?" I asked.

"Something like that. Can you recite that monologue, El Gato?"

"Piece of cake," he said. Which might not have meant what Gustave thought it meant.

"Excellent! The stage manager will soon escort you to the stage and lead El Gato to the star pedestal to recite Shakespeare."

"Maybe he should recite from *Nine Lives to Live* instead," I suggested. "I was in that movie."

Gustave glared at me. "I don't think so. Now, while El Gato's delivering his marvelous monologue, kung fu cat . . ."

"It's Rosie."

"Marvelous. Rosie, you climb up to the flying trapeze with Bruiser. Three minutes into El Gato's monologue, you both swoop down, with Bruiser holding Rosie by her legs. Rosie reaches down and swipes El Gato's hat. Can you do that?"

"I can do that!" said Rosie.

"Bruiser also can!"

"Stunt cat, here's where you come in . . ."

You roll to the center of the stage atop a giant ball + say, "I'll rescue your hat, El Gato!" Rosie says, "You want this hat? Go get it!" and throws the hat into the ring of fire. Stunt cat, you leap *into* the flaming hot ring, catch the hat with your teeth, and land safely in the net below. Then I'll give you $1,000.

Giant ball? Ring of fire? Teeth? Sweat began pooling inside my ears. I had hoped my stunt cat days were over. And yet . . . one thousand dollars!

Rosie, on the other hand, was jumping up and down. "This circus scene will be awesome in our movie!"

Yes, our movie, a movie starring me. Not as a stunt cat, but as Mr. Puffball, himself.

Big difference!

Soon the stage manager came for us. "You need something sparkly." She plunked a jeweled turban onto Rosie's head. We followed her out. Acrobats dressed as Buckingham Palace guards flew overhead. The stage set was London in miniature, with a tiny London Bridge, a little Big Ben, and a very realistic Ye Olde Fish & Chip Shoppe.

As El Gato assumed his spot on the star pedestal, the audience chanted, "El Gato! El Gato!" Except one she-cat who yelled, "Cumbercat! O, Cumbercat! Wherefore art thou Cumbercat?"

Stage left, Rosie ascended a rope ladder behind Bruiser while holding a movie camera. El Gato began reciting:

Not exactly Shakespeare. But the audience didn't seem to mind. One cat yelled, "Say 'I'm looking for the guy who shot my paw!'" A tiny kitten with a clown nose jumped onto El Gato's shoulder and whispered in his ear. Cute touch.

Meanwhile, I made a quick checklist of all I had to do to earn $1,000 and called it:

ALL I HAD TO DO TO EARN $1,000

1. Mount the giant rubber ball decorated with the British flag.
2. Balance and roll to the center of the ring.
3. Watch Bruiser and Rosie sail down on the flying trapeze and snatch El Gato's hat.
4. Wait for Rosie to inquire, "You want this hat?" then toss it into the ring of fire.
5. Launch myself into the flaming ring.
6. Rescue the hat in my teeth.
7. Land safely in safety net.
8. Accept applause with deep bow.
9. Collect $1,000.

And then it was time. A strong cat slid me to the top of the giant ball. Check. After a moment of flailing, I found my balance. Check.

I rolled to the center. Check.

Bruiser and Rosie soared down. Check.

Rosie reached for El Gato's hat. No check. Because instead of El Gato's monologue, we heard "Hello? Fish and chips? Anybody?" coming from inside the sets. He'd been lured by the siren song of the Ye Olde Fish & Chip Shoppe. So there was no El Gato hat to steal nor any El Gato to be seen.

So this happened:

1. Rosie tosses her turban.

2. I launch after it.

3. Bruiser knocks the turban . . .

4. . . . into the fire.

5. The flaming hat drops onto the flammable ball.

6. The terrible thing happens.

The ball combusted, the audience oohed, the acrobats flew away, and the ceiling sprinklers sprayed into action. The *pop!* and *sizzle!* along with the smell of burning rubber made my stomach curl up like a deflated ball.

Gustave made his way toward us through the downpour. He did not look happy. "Now you've done it. The Queen of England was in the audience. And Her Majesty did not find the show marvelous."

Gustave ushered us offstage, down the halls, and out of the theater.

"Do we still get our money?" Rosie asked.

Gustave's face softened. "Of course you get your money." He took out a huge wad of cash and counted out ten ten-dollar bills.

"I'm no math genius," I said, "but I believe that's one hundred dollars. You said one thousand dollars."

"That is one thousand dollars. Minus nine hundred in damages. Now get out of here before I send in the angry clowns."

"Send in the what?" I asked.

Klown on Board

"**D**id somebody say clown?"

"Aren't you the kitten who told me to try the fish and chips?" asked El Gato.

"Not me," he said.

"Hey, small cat," said Bruiser. "Something you needing?"

"I needing to be with El Gato and am in no way associated with Benedict Cumbercat."

Rosie looked the kitten up and down. "He must be

with Cirque du Soleil. Now let's get back to our cross-country road trip. We got some awesome footage and one hundred dollars!"

"Even though it didn't end perfectly," I said, "I can't wait to tell Chet we were in Cirque du Soleil."

"Big whoop," said a small, pesky voice. "I've been with Cirque since I was a kitten. You should see what I can do with a bungee cord."

It was that irritating kitten again.

"Are you following us?" There was the van. And there was the kitten, blocking our path with his hypnotic charm.

"You have to go back to Cirque now, cutie," Rosie explained gently.

"No way, José," said the kitten. "Once you hear my story, you won't dream of making me go back." He jumped on top of the van.

I grabbed for him, but Rosie swatted my paw down. *Ouch.* That hurt my ego!

"Picture an adorable kitten surrounded by siblings who don't understand Shakespeare. Or the beauty of breaking out in song."

"I hope this isn't another one of those stories about a kitten who dreams of stardom," I said. "Boring!"

Rosie shushed me, and the kitten continued. "One day, Mom says"—the kitten made his voice extra squeaky and momlike—"'Darlings, it's Free Kitten Day at the circus. Let's go!'"

He acted out the scene, running around like a whole herd of kittens. "'Yay!' 'Hooray!' 'I love circus!' say the kittens. They go and meet the smelly Mr. Gustave."

Now the kitten did an impressive Gustave imitation, putting on a scowly face and muttering:

"'What do you marvelous cats want?'"

He switched back to his squeaky voice to say:

"'We want to see the circus. Free Kitten Day?'"

Back to Gustave voice:

"'Free Kitten Day means kittens work at the circus for free all day.'"

Back to Mom voice:

"'Get away from the bad cat, children. We're going home.'"

Now the kitten put his own face back on. "This is the part of the story where my life changes forever, which may be too intense for some listeners. Are you sure you want to hear the rest?"

"They all went home, except the handsomest kitten, the one who always dreamed of show business. That kitten, Pickles, me, I'm Pickles, hid inside a clown car. In a few hours or maybe minutes, Konzo the Klown opened the door. I jumped out and yelled, 'Surprised?!' From that moment on, Konzo the Klown loved me, the talented kitten, and taught me all things klown. And when the time came for me to be an adorable little klown on an itsy-bitsy tricycle, everybody loved me. And I loved applause. And circus peanuts. I was happy. Until the day Konzo took me to an El Gato movie called *Nine Lives to Live* . . ."

ME: I was in that!

PICKLES: Not! Anyway, now all Pickles wanted was to be near El Gato. And here he is. So here I am. The end.

"El Gato, give the kitten your autograph so we can leave."

"Don't leave me!" said Pickles. "I'm not a bad kitty!"

"But Pickles," said Rosie. "We're on a cross-country road trip. Maybe you could come to Hollywood when you're older. . . ."

El Gato pulled me by the ear—ouch!—into a mini-huddle. "Don't you see, Mr. Puffball? This kitten could add youthful appeal to our buddy movie demo reel, like Ms. Bossypaws wants!"

I liking this little one.

WEIGHTS LIFTINGS RULE

I glanced over at the kitten.

Sigh.

"He really is adorable," said Rosie. "A kitten on our trip could be fun."

Let's face it. Kittens on trips are not fun. They're not even fun at home. But I was powerless against the tsunami of cuteness that was Pickles.

Ten minutes Later...

Back on the open highway, I learned Pickles' greatest skill: getting on my nerves.

PICKLES: I have to pee.

ME: But you went five minutes ago.

PICKLES: Then I dared myself to drink a whole bottle of soda. Now I REALLY have to go.

ME: Just hold it.

PICKLES: Can't.

ME: Is it raining?

PICKLES: Good news! I don't have to go anymore.

Grrr.

PICKLES: Let's sing. *Ninety-nine bottles of milk*
on the wall, ninety-nine bottles of milk!
If one of those bottles should happen to
fall . . . (*Pause.*) Can I get some milk here?!

Grrr.

Unfortunately, El Gato thought Pickles was the best thing since trout jerky.

Giant eye roll.

We drove for what felt like an eternity (at least thirty minutes) until I pulled up next to this sign:

"Hooray!" said Pickles, bounding out of the van.

"Photo op!" said El Gato.

Rosie snapped pictures. "Say 'cheese'!"

Fun? Kind of. But now it was time to get down to the business we call "demo reel at one of America's favorite landmarks."

What could possibly go wrong?

GOOD POSINGS, FRIENDIE.
THANKS.
THANKS.
I Try.
HOOVER DAM
MOST
THE WORLD
BIG AND STRONG.
A LOT OF
KEEPING

I WANT Cheese.
Dam
IT'S OURS, see?!
ours
AM I IN THE SHOT?

Slippery When Wet

Stuck right between Nevada and Arizona, the Hoover Dam is the world's fifty-ninth largest hydroelectric generation system. Meaning it mysteriously turns the power of water into electricity. (Wow!) The dam is a 726-foot-high, 1,244-foot-long curved structure made from over three million cubic yards of concrete before your grandparents were born. It's got a monument to the more than one hundred cats who died during its construction and a plaque to honor one brave dog who helped with inspections. It has tile designs based on Native American art, sculptures, giant concrete pipes, and a gift shop with Hoover Dam snow globes.

"More important," added Rosie, after we learned these factoids, "this is where they filmed that scene from *Supercat* where the Hoover Dam bursts."

"Could we make the dam burst for the demo reel?"
I asked.

"Unlikely," said El Gato. "But if I don't find a litter box soon, I'm going to burst."

So I joined El Gato for a quick litter box stop, and
then Rosie and I talked about how our scene should
go down:

1. Walk to the center of the dam along its crest
   (like we were doing).
2. Stage to look like El Gato falls over the side.
   Rosie explained she could do it with angles
   and mirrors. (I insisted we get clearance
   from Hoover Dam security first.)

3. I "bravely" "rescue" him as he's "dangling over the edge."
4. Add hysterical dialogue (i.e., "Why are your paws so slippery? Have you been eating sardines packed in oil again?").

But when we got halfway across the dam:

Rosie whipped out her megaphone. "Pickles, you're not even in this scene!"

Meanwhile, El Gato got busy entertaining the tourists:

"Maybe let small cat do climb ladders," said Bruiser. "Could be excitement!"

"I'm willing to give it a shot, no pun intended," said Rosie, setting up her camera. "I wonder what this button does?"

Pickles climbed, against my better judgment. This wasn't youthful energy—it was pure insanity. When he whipped out a bungee cord, it was a national disaster in the making.

"No, no, no!" I said to the wind (because nobody else was listening).

"Okay," said Rosie. "Now . . . *action!*"

Hoover Dam security guards were running directly toward us. Tourists were pointing up at Pickles, who was waving the bungee cord, yelling, "Here's your scene!"

"Let's start rolling before the cops get here!" yelled Rosie.

Suddenly I knew there was only one cat who could stop full-on shenanigans from erupting. Me.

As I climbed up, Pickles was securing the bungee cord to the turret overlooking the Colorado River far below. "Mr. Puffball, you're a stunt cat. Let's do this thing!"

"You're forgetting something very important," I said.

"What's that?" asked Pickles.

"I'm the star here!" Then I lunged for him, lost my balance, and fell.

"Wait for me!" Pickles leapt onto my back and wrapped the bungee cord around us both.

"Whee!" And off we hurled, into the abyss, plunging at lightning speed toward the Colorado River. As the bungee cord stretched to its limit, my paws grazed the frigid water. And then: *Boing!* We sprang back up!

A giant crowd of tourists, Rosie and her camera among them, peered over the edge, gasping with horror and delight and snapping pics.

Hurtling back over the edge, we slammed onto the cement bridge with an alarming *thwack!*

"Radical!" Pickles said, sitting on my nearly deflated chest.

Then the guards were on us like kittens on a yarn ball, pulling out walkie-talkies, shiny handcuffs, and other Implements of Security.

Who would you believe? An itty-bitty kitty with ginormous eyes? Or the cat in the awesome bow tie who was probably some kind of crazed thrill-seeker?

El Gato was no help at all. He shook his head and said, "Some cats will do anything for attention." He pulled me up off the ground, put his paw around my shoulder, and turned to the crowd. "Photo op! El Gato with the cat who bungeed off the Hoover Dam!"

Then Rosie popped up with her megaphone. "And . . . cut!"

Bruiser slapped me on the back. "You crazy cat! I like!"

Two guards grabbed me like I was a criminal. "Time to take this criminal to the hoosegow." Also known as: the big house, the cooler, jail.

It looked like curtains for our young hero.

"I have a plan," Bruiser whispered.

I thought of the possible success rate of any plan Bruiser could devise on such short notice:

Projected effectiveness of hastily conceived plan involving weight lifting, bench pressing, speed walking, arm wrestling, discus throwing, shark riding, loud talking in broken English, or anything else from Bruiser's skill set, as a pie chart

Then he did something else.

"I feel crazy action coming! Bungee jumpee . . . with no rope! Olden school!" Bruiser caught my eye and winked. He climbed up to the edge of the dam, yelling, "Come get me, copters!"

The guards dropped everything (meaning me) and ran to him. "Halt! You can't do that!"

"Bruiser tuff like bull! Run, Puffyball, I catching you later!" Then he launched himself into a perfect swan dive.

"Thanks, Bruiser!" I bellowed, glancing over the side as he soared toward the Colorado River. He'd be fine. He was Bruiser. "Let's skedaddle!"

In minutes we were back in the van. All except Pickles, who'd been mesmerized by Bruiser's diving exploit. Now Pickles sprinted toward us, yelling, "Roll down the window! Go, go, go!!" The guards were right behind him, so I stepped on the gas.

Whoosh! Something flew by my whiskers. *Wham!*— the kitten was buckling up next to me.

"Not bad, kid," I said. "You'd make a good stunt cat. But I'm still mad at you for that bungee episode. Don't you realize we've got to stick with the script?"

Then he laid his head on Rosie and immediately fell asleep, which brought on a big round of *awww*s. He was adorable. He was photogenic. He made for good cinema.

The little stinker.

A New Set of Wheels

"Next stop, the Grand Canyon," said Rosie as we crossed into Arizona the next day.

"How about the Mall of America?" asked Pickles. "They have rides!"

"And a food court!" said El Gato.

"And balloons . . . ," said Pickles.

This went on for hours, until, finally, we reached the Grand Canyon.

"I'm the director," said Rosie, "and this is our location for the next scene: Buddies Leap the Grand Canyon."

"But isn't it very, very, very, very, very, very, very wide?" asked Pickles.

"Welcome to the magic of moviemaking," said Rosie. "Chet taught me creative editing techniques in his lesson 'Creative Editing Techniques.' Here's how it will happen—as a list à la Mr. Puffball."

A LIST (À LA MR. PUFFBALL) OF HOW TO MAKE IT LOOK LIKE TWO CATS ARE LEAPING OVER THE GRAND CANYON

1. After a good running start, El Gato and Mr. Puffball jump toward the canyon.
2. Cut. They land safely at the edge.
3. I pan slowly across the entire canyon while . . . (see step four)
4. Mr. Puffball and El Gato scream things like "I hope we don't die!" and "If we do, I'm gonna kill you!" or something equally hilarious. Cut.
5. We stroll to the other side. They jump like they just landed after leaping over the canyon, with lots of panting, sweatiness, and *phews*.
6. Later, I edit in footage of their paws dangling over my pan of the canyon. The end.

"Hey," said El Gato as we walked toward the canyon. "We made an astronaut movie with Catt Damon here a few months ago because it looks exactly like

Mars. How 'bout we make this scene Buddies Leap over a Grand Crater on Mars? Ms. Bossypaws wants the future, remember?"

"Forget about Mars!" said Rosie. "Obey your director!"

El Gato and I positioned ourselves a few paws from the edge of one of the seven natural wonders of the world. The Grand Canyon averages ten miles across, one mile deep, and 277 miles long, and the rock found at its bottom is almost two billion years old (that's older than your great-great-great-grandmother!). It's been featured in lots of movies, including *Supercat* and *Transformers*. I looked into the vast depths and breathed in the ancient stratified-rock-dust-filled air. Wow!

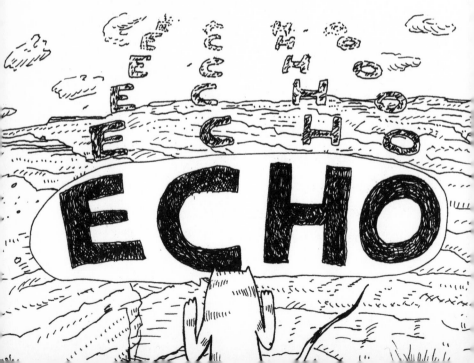

"Okay, actors," said Rosie. "I want you to ad lib. And . . . *action*!"

"Add lip?" I said. "You mean be sassy?"

"Ad lib. Invent dialogue to fit the scene. First, get into character. El Gato, you're the buddy who'll do anything for a delicious meal. Mr. Puffball, you're the buddy who wants to be famous, no matter what it takes."

"Am I the buddy who beatboxes?" asked Pickles.

"Maybe later. Now—quiet on the set! And . . . *action*!"

"It's a mighty long way across, buddy," said El Gato, peering across the canyon. "Isn't there a diner on this side of the canyon?"

"Perhaps, buddy. But they've got the best onion rings on the other side."

"Can we really jump all the way across the Grand Canyon?"

"Of course! We're cats, aren't we?"

"Yeah, we're cats. Not kangaroos."

"Cut!" yelled Pickles.

Rosie came out from behind the camera. "Hey! I'm the only one who yells *cut*!'"

"But I like to yell 'cut!' too," said Pickles.

Eye roll!

Just then a tour bus screeched to a stop nearby.

"Pickles," said Rosie. "Go over to the nice cats on that tour bus, explain that we're shooting a film, and politely request they be quiet. Okay?"

"Yes way, José!" He ran off. And quickly returned.

"Pickles!" yelled Rosie happily. "You brought props! I'm making you Head Prop Cat."

"I love skateboards!" said El Gato.

Double eye roll.

"Fine," I said. "Pickles, hand over the skateboards."

"No way," yelled Pickles. "I brought the props, so I'm in this scene."

"No way!"

"Way," said El Gato. "Pickles is the future. He should be in this scene."

"As your director," said Rosie, "I agree. He'll add youthful energy to the opening shot."

BUDDIES LEAP THE GRAND CANYON take two! And... ACTION!

"Action!" said Pickles, rolling up on one skateboard with the other one tucked under his arm. "Dudes, if you're gonna jump the Big Hole, you're gonna need these."

"Cut!" said Rosie. "Good job, Pickles. El Gato and Mr. Puffball, take it from when El Gato said, 'Yeah, we're cats. Not kangaroos.' And . . . action!"

"We may not be kangaroos, buddy, but thanks to that kitten dude"—I restrained a giant eye roll—"we've got something those crazy Aussies don't have." I held up the skateboards. "Boards."

"Radical!"

We mounted the boards, rolled from the edge, and pivoted, all in sync. "We are rebels!" I yelled.

And off we zoomed. *Zoom!* As a trained stunt cat, I knew I could stop at the exact right moment. But what about El Gato?

"Hold on, buddy, I'll save you!" El Gato was dangling from a root about ten paws down. "Pickles," I called, "the bungee cord!"

"You've got to save him!" screamed Rosie. "Or we'll never finish the demo reel!"

"I'm on it," I said, securing the cord around myself. "Hold this end, Rosie. You help too, Pickles. Lower me into the canyon, I'll grab El Gato, and when I say the word, pull with all your might."

"I got tons of might!" said Pickles.

I looked him in the eye and put a confidence-building paw on his shoulder. "Buddy, I like your cat-titude."

I hurried to the edge, checked the strength of the cord, and descended into the canyon while Pickles yelled, "I'm using all my might, Mr. Puffball."

Soon the big guy and I were whisker to whisker. He let out a quiet whimper. "I got you, buddy." I wrapped my paws around his belly. "Okay!" I called out. "Pull us up!" We ascended slowly, up, up, and up. We were only one paw length from the edge when the line jerked, and we began slipping back down. I dug my paws into the sandy limestone slope, but it crumbled away like it was a billion years old or so. We fell as far as the root El Gato had been clutching earlier. I grabbed for it, my paw grazing only the tip. I swung my tail to gain momentum, reached again, and this time, *bingo!* I had the root firmly in paw, and it held.

For two seconds. *Snap!*

We slammed into the canyon wall—ouch!—and descended into the chasm once more. Up we went. Then back down. Then nothing. We hung in space, spinning over our doom.

"Don't look down!" I told El Gato.

"What? I can't hear you over the pounding drum!"

"Can we get fish and chips after this? I'd like to think we'll get fish and chips."

Then came the sound of a voice. A British voice. "Did somebody say fish and chips?" I glanced up—*gasp!*—Benedict Cumbercat's face was looking right at us! "Oh dear, someone's demo reel's gone brilliantly wrong."

"You!"

"No need to thank me. America's favorite actor is happy to help."

"El Gato is America's favorite actor."

"I don't think so, mates." He turned to the tourists. "Who here loves me?" A huge cheer went up. Somebody yelled, "Do Furlock Holmes!"

"Elementary, my dear Watson." Another cheer went up. "Now who wants to see me rescue endangered cats?"

Suddenly we felt an upward tug as Benedict pulled us up. "This is a job for Furlock Holmes!" he said. We gradually ascended and were dragged over the rocky edge. We crawled as far as possible from the chasm that had nearly claimed our bones forever to the sound of the crowd chanting, "Furlock! Furlock!"

"I don't love skateboards anymore," said El Gato.

"Pickles, what happened?" I asked. "Did you let go of the bungee cord?"

Pickles rubbed up against Rosie. "He dropped it because Benedict Cumbercat called him over. What were you two talking about, anyway?"

"Umm . . . how to make it in show business?"

"Where'd he go?" I asked, raising my paws for a round of fisticuffs.

"He was carried off by a busload of tourists," said Rosie.

I lowered my paws. "Pickles, I trusted you. And you let me down."

"Let's finish this scene," I said. "And then . . ."

"And then we eat," said El Gato.

We couldn't find a fish and chips shop in the middle of Arizona. But we did find this place:

Which is where we found a poster tacked up by the fates themselves, guiding us to our next buddy movie demo reel location.

The Rodeo to Ruin

"*F*ocus, cats!" said Rosie. "We're running out of time, and we need to get to Wyoming. This rodeo's got everything we need for a killer demo reel scene: prancing horses, cowboy suits, clowns, lariats, and corn dogs. Tonight we rest up. Tomorrow we've got to be at that rodeo. Mr. Puffball, make it so."

Fourteen hours later . . .

Welcome, Buckaroos! to the world's Biggest, bestest, most Wild-westest, hoof-thunderin' Rodeo!

COW-CAT PARKING ONLY!! ALL oThers will be Hog-tied!!!

We hopped out and saw a huge line of cats waiting to get into the rodeo.

"We've got our crowd," said Rosie. "Let's go. The scene: two buddies putting on a show for genuine rodeo cats. The buddies are city cats who think they understand rodeo folk but don't at all. High jinks ensue."

"As you know," I said, "I can ride a genuine horse. If he's properly trained."

"I can eat corn dogs by the dozen," said El Gato.

"And I can be the rodeo clown," said Pickles.

"Set up the stage," said Rosie. "I'll get my equipment and rev up the crowd."

I pushed together several bales of hay, and El Gato and I climbed up.

"Rodeo folk," megaphoned Rosie. "Welcome to a pre-rodeo show you'll never forget. Let's hear lots of whooping and hollering for two buddies on a cross-country road trip visiting the American heartland. And . . . *action!*"

"Howdy, you all down-home cats of Wyoming and thereabouts," I said, slipping effortlessly into rodeo lingo. "We're a couple of green-horned cow-felines from over yonder Hollywood way."

"El Gato," hissed Rosie. "Say something!"

"Yee-haw! Yippee-i-o-ki-ay!"

Murmurs of "El Gato!" and "Some other cat" spread through the crowd. I held my paws high. "Is there a trained horse here who wants to be in our demo reel?"

Somebody yelled, "El Gato! Say 'I'm looking fer the guy who shot my paw!'" A cheer went up from the crowd.

Rosie megaphoned, "Quiet on the set!"

But El Gato was eating up the attention. "I'm looking fer the guy who shot my paw," he said.

"Stay in character!" I whispered. "You're not El Gato, you're buddy number one."

"The camera's rolling!" said Rosie.

"Yippee!" yelled Pickles, leaping from out of nowhere onto our hay-bale stage.

This ain't my first rodeo! Let's get this SHINDIG STARTED!

A horse started moving through the crowd toward us. "There's our scene!" I yelled, waving my arms. "Over here, Mr. Horsey!" The horse galloped closer. On his back was a she-cat in a cowboy hat.

"Did somebody say demo reel?" said the she-cat.

"Has this horse been in anything I might have seen?" I said.

Suddenly the she-cat swooped down, scooped up me, El Gato, and Pickles one at a time, and plunked us onto the horse's back.

"Cut!" yelled Rosie. "What's going on here?"

"Calico Sue's going on!" said Pickles.

"I'm the director," said Rosie. "And you need to get down right now so we can plan the next scene!"

Calico Sue slid us all off the horse—*bam!*—and said: "I know about your buddy movie demo reel. It's all over the celebrity gossip magazines."

"And since we love celebrities so much," said Calico Sue, "I'm fixin' to get you the biggest, bestest, buddiest scene of your life."

"A runaway horse scene?" I asked.

"While I make the world laugh as the adorable clown?" asked Pickles.

"We were hoping for a lariat scene with gleaming spurs," said Rosie.

"And funnel cakes," said El Gato.

"I got something even better," said Calico Sue, as she waved over a camera-cat from a local TV station. "Big announcement, everybody! El Gato is gonna be our guest movie star in today's bull-riding contest."

El Gato grabbed his guts and squeaked, "Bull riding?"

"Just like you done in *Cow-Cats & Aliens.*"

"But in my movies, I use . . . ," started El Gato, but Calico Sue grabbed his cheeks and squeezed.

Are you gonna tell your RODEO FANS You're one of those LiLY-Livered skeerdy-PANTS WHO CALLS A STUNT CAT EVERY TIME You're 'Bout to get Yer PAWS Mussed?

NO, MA'AM.

"Good," she said. "Then follow me."

"Give us a minute," said Rosie, pulling us into an actors' huddle.

"I don't want to die," whispered El Gato.

"You won't," whispered Rosie. "You and Mr. Puffball can do your usual switcheroo. He puts on your outfit, and he rides the bull."

"No thank you!" I said.

"But Mr. Puffball," said Rosie, "a bull-riding scene would give us the edge we need to steal back the buddy movie! This is your ticket to stardom!"

"Excellent point, Rosie, but . . . do I have to?"

Just then a firm paw tapped my shoulder.

"I almost forgot to tell you," said Calico Sue. "If El Gato can stay on the bull for twelve seconds, he gets one thousand dollars."

"Think of all the film equipment we could buy with that money," squeaked Rosie.

I looked into her big eyes and knew I couldn't let her down. And anyway, once a stunt cat, always a stunt cat, even if I didn't want to be a stunt cat anymore.

"I'll do it," I said. "I mean, El Gato will do it!"

El Gato puffed out his chest. "I am very brave."

Calico Sue steered us into the giant arena. Around the center ring was an audience of floor-to-ceiling cats in cowboy hats. The place smelled like bull poop and nachos. Rosie and Pickles took front-row seats. "I have to use the litter box first," El Gato said, and his eyes shifted toward me. "Don't you have to use the litter box first, Mr. Puffball, buddy?"

"Now that's friendship," said Calico Sue. "I'll be waiting for you boys right here."

We found the restrooms and quickly switched outfits. Then El Gato joined Rosie and Pickles as Calico Sue dragged me to the center of the dusty arena. From inside the bull pens (aka chutes) lining the perimeter, the bulls bucked wildly. I let out a quiet groan. "Man up!" she said, before bellowing into her microphone.

Chants of "El Gato! El Gato! El Gato!" went up from the stands. Rosie was set up to film. I barely heard her yell, "Quiet on the set!" over the din.

"That's right, pardners!" boomed Calico Sue. "El Gato's here to ride a bull. Should we let him ride Ferdinand?"

"No!" shouted the crowd.

"How 'bout Buckey?"

"No!"

"Then I reckon he'll have to ride . . . Bodacious!"

"Is Bodacious in the Screen Actors Guild?" asked Rosie.

The crowd roared, and I took a deep, confidence-building breath. I'd ridden atop moving trains and ill-tempered horses. I'd wrestled a shark. And an alligator.

It's not like I had to tap-dance on the bull. It's not like I had to sing "The Star-Spangled Banner" on the bull. I didn't even have to look cheerful on the bull. All I had to do was not get thrown off for twelve seconds.

I could do that!

Calico Sue walked me to the bull chute. "Stay

strong, El Gato. Bodacious is a tough son of a gun, a traditional bucker who'll give you a north-south ride like a seesaw cyclone. Stay away from the hurricane deck, never touch the flank strap, and whatever you do, don't get hooked."

"Could you rephrase that?"

"Listen, Tenderfoot, I can't explain bull riding to you all in a minute. Just hold on and hold on tight. Squeeze with your leg muscles and use your upper-body strength."

"What if I haven't got any upper-body strength?"

We approached the fence, and she pointed to a sign.

"These rodeo folk don't mess around," said Calico Sue.

NO stunt cats.
NO exceptions.
OR WE PROMISE YOU
A WHOLE HEAP O' TROUBLE.

"Yes, ma'am," I said as she yanked open the gate. And there I was, face-to-face with the biggest, maddest, most nose-ring-wearing-est bull ever.

Back in the Saddle Again

Calico Sue pushed me inside. "Meet Bodacious," she said, and slammed the gate shut.

"Greetings, Bodacious. I'm the world-famous celebrity El Gato. You may have seen me in such movies as . . ." Bodacious snorted so viciously I expected steam to come out of his nostrils, like you see in old cartoons. He pawed the ground like a lunatic and made a noise that sounded like "Quiet, you."

Cowhands scooped me up and plopped me onto Bodacious' back. I grabbed the bull rope, which is what they call the rope you clutch while begging for mercy. "Hey, big fella," I said, "have you ever heard the phrase 'Give peace a chance'?"

And *bam!* The gate flew open.

Dear reader, please do me a favor. Count out twelve seconds. One Mississippi. Two Mississippi. That's only two Mississippis! And already my spine has been jolted a trillion times in directions here-tofore unknown to me. My neck is whipping back and forth so hard my head's about to snap clean off. Sweat is pouring out of every part of me while I cling desperately to a bull determined to throw me to Timbuktu, wherever that is. On my third *Mississippi*, we pass by Rosie.

In that moment, a perplexing mini-drama played out:

1. A tall, slender cat with a cowboy hat pulled down low tapped Pickles on the shoulder and held out a red bandanna.

2. Pickles glanced up nervously and shook his head no.

3. The slender cat's lips moved angrily as he shoved the red bandanna at Pickles. Pickles took it.

4. The tall cat slipped back into the crowd, never to be seen again for a while.

5. Pickles leaned over the wall between the stands and the arena, the red bandanna dangling redly from his paws.

Boy, was that bandanna red. You could say scarlet. Or crimson. Or ruby. Either way, it was the exact color that bulls hate.

"No, Pickles!" I yelled at the same moment that Bodacious ground to a halt, nearly throwing me off.

"Now you're in focus!" yelled Rosie. "Bodacious, your character is a very angry bull. And . . . action!"

He ignored Rosie, glared at the bandanna, lowered his head, and pawed the ground maniacally. "He's gonna charge!" I yelled.

But he wasn't going to stop. We were going to hit. Hard. I would go flying and probably land right in the churro kiosk. Good-bye, money. Good-bye, dignity. Good-bye, not being inside a vat of boiling churro oil.

We were inches from impact when Pickles dropped the bandanna, leapt out of the stands, yelled, "I can't do it!" and landed on the bull. Pickles grabbed the bull's ear and leaned over it. I saw his tiny lips moving.

"Now we both die," I despaired. "And I'm so young."

But, as you may have guessed, I did not die. The bull resumed his bucking, but not quite so furiously. Pickles was in front of me now, holding the rope and staring into my eyes. "Seven seconds down. Five to go," he said. "You got this, Mr. Puffball."

He was right. I did got it. The crowd counted off the final seconds: "Nine! Ten! Eleven! And twelve!"

And the bull stopped. Yes, I got thrown. But my bones were intact. Most of my blood remained inside my body. And the crowd went hog wild.

Calico Sue rushed toward me with a huge wad of cash and a microphone. Rosie and El Gato were right behind her. Calico Sue handed me the prize money and held out the mic so I could say a few words. Rosie threw her paws around me. "I got some amazing footage, Mr. Puffball!"

"What did she call him?" said a voice in the crowd.

Pickles jumped on my shoulder and whipped off my mask and hat. "Look, everybody! This guy's Mr. Puffball, the world's greatest stunt cat!" His words echoed through the arena.

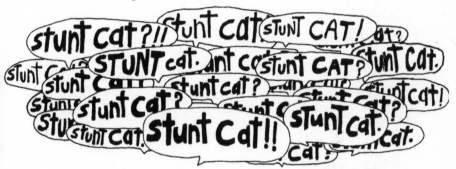

"That stunt cat's trying to hornswoggle us," somebody yelled. "Get him!"

A mob of furious cow-cats leapt from the stands and stormed our way. "Let's vamoose!" I yelled. Rosie, El Gato, and I started racing for the exit, but Pickles whistled, and as fast as you can say Bodacious, Bodacious was beside us. "Hop on up, everybody."

The bull could talk!

Bodacious snorted and drove us through the exit doors while the crowd yelled:

"We'll get you, stunt cat!"

And I yelled, "Hang on, pardners!"

And Pickles yelled, "This way, Bodacious!"

And Rosie yelled, "The camera's getting jostled!"

And El Gato yelled, "Funnel cakes!"

Bodacious raced to the van and stopped on a dime somebody had dropped in the parking lot. We all fell off, except Pickles. He grabbed the cash out of my paws, counted out some bills, and handed them to Bodacious, who turned around to charge the approaching mob.

We scrambled into the van. I stepped on it, and we took off. And if you think this is the moment when the heroes cheer for joy because they're finally home free, guess again.

Calico Sue had us lassoed!

"On it!" said Pickles. He climbed out and sawed through the rope with his tiny razor-sharp claws. Impressive!

"Thanks, Pickles," I said as we sped out of town. "By the way, who was that guy who gave you the red bandanna?"

His supersize eyes shifted nervously. "A guy who was giving away bandannas."

"And what did you say to that bull?" asked Rosie.

"I told him I worked with his cousin Tauro when he was a guest star at Cirque du Soleil. Plus I promised him three hundred dollars of the prize money. Bodacious wants to buy a new nose ring."

"A nose ring costs three hundred dollars?" asked El Gato.

"He's getting one for his wife, too," said Pickles.

Now for Something Completely Different

"**H**i, I'm El Gato. You may remember me from such movies as *Cow-Cats & Aliens* and *Hairy Pawter and the Goblet of Fur*. But there's another side of me you may not know. The side with his own foodie TV show. Welcome to:

EL GATO 'EATS RIGHT' ACROSS AMERICA!

Some cats warn that fried foods are fattening. Do they expect me to NOT eat onion rings, even when I'm in an ACTUAL onion ring ranch? That can't be right!

What's the main benefit of drinking milk? A milk moustache. Right on!

Do presidents rule the nation by eating salad? Not when faced with White House—quality french fries (a food widely considered to be one of our fundamental rights).

I know the sign says no snacking, but it's a low-calorie, high-fiber food. Anyway, I only bit one side—the right.

Is it wrong to drive thru a donut hole? When we finally got unstuck, we bought a van-ful of donuts, which made everything all right.

Every restaurant should have a theme. Can you guess the theme of Barnacle Bill's Scallywag Food Shack?

"That's my foodie report from the road! Back to you, Mr. Puffball."

END EL GATO SEGMENT

BACK TO OUR STORY:

Our bodies need food. And our van needs . . .
oops!

That's right, we ran out of gas. I deployed my wits
to once again save the day.

Then it was time to follow the map to Chicago.
Look out, Chicago!

Seriously, look out.

Danger Ahead

"Rosie, I know we're on a tight schedule, but can we please find a way to trick Benedict Cumbercat into looking ridiculous for our demo reel?"

"Is he definitely on the set for *Bonnie and Clawed*?"

"Yes, he's there today! And Chet asked us to be extras in the bank heist scene."

"Perfect!" said Rosie. "We'll go straight to the Bank of Chicago, and—"

"And Mr. Puffball punches Cumbercat in the nose from behind!" Pickles piped up uninvited. "Or we put this on him." Pickles held up his old clown nose. "It smells weird."

"Were you sitting on it again?" I asked.

"OR, as I was saying," continued Rosie, "we go to the bank. Pretend we don't know about the movie . . ."

"Oh, like we think it's a real bank heist?" I asked.

"Great idea! I'll grab Benedict, say, 'I'm placing you under arrest' . . . Wait a minute, what's this?"

I followed the detour sign and pulled up in front of a bank just in time to see this:

"Those bags look so fake," said Rosie. "And Chet's always telling me it's all in the details."

"He did an excellent job concealing the cameras, though," I said.

I hopped out of the van and strolled up to the car ahead of us. Inside was a nervous-looking cat. "Hey, buddy, you on this gig?" I asked. He gasped, stepped on the gas, and peeled out. Must have been camera shy.

Running toward us were the actors who were playing bank robbers. One of them said, "Hey! Where's our getaway car?"

Aha, I thought, *here's our chance to pretend we don't know what's happening. Cumbercat must be right behind them.* I threw up my paws and said, "Oh no! Scary gangsters! I hope you don't use our van as the getaway car!" Then I stage-whispered, "It's okay. We know Chet. And we're pranking Cumbercat. Where is he, by the way?"

The three actors looked at me strangely. But when I opened the van doors, they shrugged and hopped in. So did I. "What now?"

"Drive, chump," said the toughest-looking one.

"Shouldn't we wait for somebody British?"

"Mr. Puffball, I'm not sure . . . ," whispered Rosie.

"Now's a good time to get out your camera," I whispered back.

One of the actors leaned forward. "Everybody, shut up. You take us to the docks, no questions asked, and nobody gets hurt. Got it, dummy?"

He was really in character! So on I drove, glancing this way and that, looking for Benedict Cumbercat.

The rude actor had a gravelly voice and smelled like hot mustard. If I didn't know I was in a movie, it would have been scary! But I kept my cool as I careened past giant trucks, zoomed under elevated train tracks, and screeched my way through the streets of Chicago. Soon an army of studio "police cars" were on my tail.

"Those 'police cars' look too modern," I said, glancing at the rearview mirror. Then I turned my eyes upward. "Helicopters? I thought this was a 1930s period piece. Somebody didn't do their research."

"Less yapping, more driving," said the tough-faced actor.

Rosie nudged me hard while Pickles pointed to the backseat, mouthing something unintelligible. I gently pushed Rosie's paw away and glared at Pickles. "Rosie, make sure you get my ace driving in a wide shot," I whispered. "Pickles, you're just an extra in this scene, so chillax."

"Zip it!" the head gangster yelled, and kicked the seat, which was a bit much. Who did he think he was?

"Just a minute, buster," I said. "Is Benedict Cumbercat in this scene or not?"

"Enough with the crazy talk, buddy. Turn here. Now!"

"Let's make this shot unforgettable! Don't worry, I'm a professional stunt cat." I turned the wheel all the way so we were spinning in a circle across three lanes of traffic. "The Chicago police force is handling traffic safety, right?"

"Cut the jokes, joker. When I say 'turn here,' you turn here. Or it's curtains for you!" said Mr. Tough Guy, jabbing me in the shoulder.

"Curtains? What do you think this is, Broadway?" I winked at Pickles. His eyes were huge. He probably had to pee. "Don't worry, little fella, I think we're almost done."

"You're the one who's done," said the mean actor. "If you don't shut it."

"Down here, jerky!" yelled the bossy cat, reaching over the backseat, grabbing the wheel, and steering us down an alley.

"I'm driving here!" I wrestled back control of the wheel.

Suddenly, a bevy of studio "police cars" and "motorcycles" swung into the alley in front of us and stopped, forming a white-and-blue barricade. "Looks like Chet hired every actor in Chicago for this scene." I hit the brakes hard.

"Is this the part where the gangsters get nabbed?" I asked.

"Not on your life," said the rude actor. He kicked the door open. "Grab El Gato," he said to his fellow actors. "That movie star could be our ticket out."

"Aren't we all movie stars?" I asked. The "gangsters" hopped out, lunged for El Gato, who was just finishing the last of the yogurt-covered mouse tails, and dragged him out by the whiskers.

"Ouch!" said El Gato. "That hurts!"

It was at that moment that I realized the horrible truth: Benedict Cumbercat was not in this scene. Then Pickles delivered an even more horrible truth. He grabbed my head and stared into my eyes. "Mr. Puffball, those dudes are not actors."

"Of course they're . . ." I glanced out the window. The police-cats had badges and megaphones and weapons. Some of them were not very attractive. They didn't look like actors. They looked like police-cats. There wasn't a camera in sight.

This wasn't a movie scene: It was a crime scene.

The police megaphoned, "You in the van. Come out with your paws up." I turned to Rosie and Pickles. The kitten said, "You two go. When those criminals come back, I'll surprise them with these bad boys."

"You're a good kitten, Pickles," I said. "But I got us into this mess. And I'm the one who should get us out."

Rosie put her paws on both our shoulders. "We'll get us out of this mess—together."

We quickly devised a plan, and called it:

THE PLAN TO SAVE EL GATO FROM THE GANGSTERS WHO WERE NOT ACTORS

1. Confuse them with flattery.

2. Distract with banter.

3. Engage in chit-chat.

4. Entrance with acting.

5. Wow with Pawter.

6. Lure with stardom.

AND THEN THE WRAP-UP:

7. Director slam.   8. Kung fu fighting.   9. Deploy the kitten!

I have to admit, Pickles was awesome. When he flew at the main gangster, the bad cat dropped his weapon and staggered back. El Gato was saved. The money would be returned. All was once again right with the world.

The police finished the job, slapping cuffs on the three villains and dragging them off to the hoosegow.

And then came my favorite part: The crowd went wild.

Diversion

"Hooray for the non-famous cats who saved El Gato!"

A huge cat pushed his way through the crowd. "Mr. Puffyball, no worries, I saving you!"

"Bruiser, how did you find us?"

"After finish bath at Hoober Dam, I spy with my little eye a certain skinny actor with strange accent." He dragged the accused out into the open. Benedict Cumbercat! "He is trouble, I feel in muscles. So I follow, and lose guy, find, follow, lose one more, and see again. He come here, so I am too."

"Your mate is barmy," said Benedict, dusting himself off. "He twisted my metacarpals."

"I never even see meta-corporal," said Bruiser.

What followed was a tense moment of tension.

The crowd moved in closer. Somebody yelled, "Is El Gato going to fight Benedict Cumbercat or what?"

Another said, "I'm not leaving until I've been entertained!"

"Into the van, everybody," said Rosie. "We're going to the Bank of Chicago to sort this whole thing out."

"And then on to New York?" asked El Gato. "I love New York!"

"Victoria Bossypaws does want some Coney Island shots," I said, cruising through downtown Chicago. "And we're practically on the East Coast already. I'm just worried about the time element."

"Even the queen loves Coney Island," said Benedict Cumbercat, as we pulled up to the Bank of Chicago and piled out of the van. "You simply must go." His intense blue-green eyes with gold specks blazed with sincerity. . . .

Okay, I admit it. I'm a Benedict Cumbercat fan. Here's but a brief look at Benedict Cumbercat's greatest roles:

His Furlock
Holmes was
pure genius.

He was
irresistably
creepy in
*PawTrek
Into
Darkness.*

He smouldered
as Smaug in
The Hobbit.

ROSIE INTERVIEWS BENEDICT CUMBERCAT!

"I'm a big fan of your work, actually," said Benedict to El Gato.

"Still," I said, "you are trying to steal our buddy movie."

"I could say you're trying to steal my buddy movie. There, I said it."

"The point is," said Rosie, holding up a firm paw, "once Ms. Bossypaws sees our awesome demo reel, Mr. Puffball and El Gato will get the gig."

"Perhaps," said Benedict with an enigmatic smile and a raised eyebrow.

Suddenly Pickles jumped onto the van.

Benedict gently removed the sign from Pickles' claws and ripped it into a million pieces. "If I'm such a baddie, would I do this?" He slid a beautiful watch off his wrist. "This belonged to my dear departed grandfather. But I want you to have it, El Gato. As evidence of my respect for your enormous"—he coughed, and it sounded like "belly"—"for your enormous talent."

Rosie trained the camera on this heartfelt moment of reconciliation in front of the Bank of Chicago. Then Chet, Kitty, and Whiskers popped into the picture.

"Rosie, you left the lens cap on again," said Chet. "Why didn't you guys come by earlier? We had to film *Bonnie and Clawed* without you."

"Long story," I said. "Now we're going to Coney Island—"

"Because of this?" asked Whiskers, holding out a newspaper:

"My sister's in a hot dog eating contest?" I said. "I thought she was a vegetarian!"

"I bet your whole family will be there," said Rosie.

"Now I really want to go," I said. "But we have to be back in Hollywood in four days!"

"Wrong," said El Gato, consulting his new watch. "This thing's got the date. According to my brand-new timepiece from my new friend Benedict, we have five days."

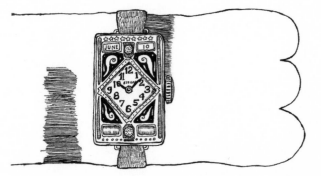

"Then let's do it!" We piled back into the van and invited Benedict Cumbercat to join us.

"I'd love to, chaps. Tell you what, you go ahead, and I'll catch up later."

"That cat sure is easy on the eyes," said Kitty as we pulled away.

"And a great actor," added Chet. "I'm glad you kids worked out your disagreement."

It was a long way to Coney Island, so we decided to play a car game.

We did stop for pizza to go. With anchovies, of course. As the van filled with the scent of anchovies, Chet told stories of yesteryear, which—*hallelujah!*—sent

Pickles to sleep and stopped him from asking twenty million questions. Soon everybody drifted off except me, because you shouldn't drive and sleep at the same time. Rosie taught me that. She'd taught me so much: how to not sideswipe other vehicles, how to avoid accidental honking, how to feed parking meters with coins, not buttons. And most of all, how to work the radio dials.

Yes, I'd become an ace driver. And somebody who knew what *ad lib* means. And a reluctant bungee jumper. And our adventure wasn't even over.

Soon Rosie woke and took the wheel. As I nodded off, visions of Coney Island rides danced in my head. We were going to have a whole world of fun!

Roller Coaster of Doom

I woke the next morning to sunrise over the Manhattan skyline. Rosie slept beside me. Her lilac scent could not overpower the vanful of stink that results from a night of seven cats and one kitten after a Chicago-style-pizza binge.

I rolled my window down, which made Rosie's eyes roll open. We quickly whispered a plan to make the most of our Coney Island visit and called it:

A PLAN TO MAKE THE MOST OF
OUR CONEY ISLAND VISIT

1. Wake everybody up for a rousing chorus of a New York–themed song (my idea).

2. Drive to Coney Island, Brooklyn. Rosie will deploy her maps to get us there. Keep singing.

3. Quickly stage an impromptu (ad libbing) scene on the world-famous Coney Island Cyclone.

4. Enjoy a speedy but meaningful family reunion. Hugs all around. Congratulate Snowball for eating the most hot dogs. (I know she'll win! She always ate all her food and most of mine.)

5. Race back to Hollywood. Astound Ms. Bossypaws with our fantastic demo reel, which is definitely better than Benedict Cumbercat's.

6. Costar in buddy movie.

7. Hello, superstardom.

We went straight to step one:

Then Rosie crinkled maps like crazy. She crinkled us through the Holland Tunnel (scary), over the Brooklyn Bridge (cool), and all the way to Coney Island (it's way at the end of the New York City map!). And there we were:

"I want to hot dog contest," said El Gato.

"We don't have time for this," said Rosie. "Your director insists we get on the Cyclone immediately, take one ride for fun, and then stage something wild and crazy and cinematic. We'll improvise."

"We wrap it up in an hour and get back here in time to see my sister win the contest," I said. "Then it's back to Hollywood."

"Now," said Rosie, hoisting her camera and megaphone, "to the Cyclone!"

"Hot dog," said El Gato.

"Okay," I said. "Bruiser, would you get us each one hot dog and meet us at the Cyclone?"

"Junk food is enemy," he said. "But when in Coney Island, do like Coney Islanders."

The Coney Island Cyclone is ginormous. Rosie set up the camera, and we got in line for one of the oldest, most fur-raising roller coasters in the universe.

"Who wants to ride?" I asked.

Everybody wanted to ride the Cyclone. To give you an idea of how fun it is, here's a chart:

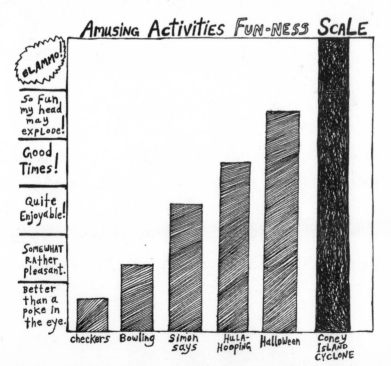

AMUSING ACTIVITIES FUN-NESS SCALE

BLAMMO!

So Fun, my head may explode!

Good Times!

Quite Enjoyable!

SOMEWHAT RATher pleasant.

Better than a poke in the eye.

checkers   Bowling   Simon says   HULA-Hooping   Halloween   Coney Island Cyclone

Rosie, Chet, Kitty, Whiskers, and I got on, but El Gato and Pickles had to wait for the next ride. The Cyclone was so very, totally, completely . . .

WHEEEEEEEEEEEEEEEEEEEEEEEEEEEEEEEEEEEEEEEEEEEEEEE

Now El Gato and Pickles got strapped in for their turn. Rosie set up the camera on the ground, and we talked actor to director about filming this next scene.

Out of the corner of my eye, I watched El Gato and Pickles laughing on the Cyclone. The sun was shining, and a lovely breeze breezed in from the Atlantic Ocean. The oldsters went to get Italian ices for everybody. (I asked for a blue, to add a touch of color to the scene.) I spotted Bruiser heading our way with a big, greasy bag of hot dogs. It was one of those magical moments when all is right with the world.

Until . . . *screech!* A horrible metal-against-metal sound filled the air, and a voice with an English accent yelled out, "England rules!" Suddenly the Cyclone ground to a halt. It was the exact moment that El Gato was turned upside down. Even from this distance, I could see the safety straps straining against his weight, as he hung suspended over an eighty-foot drop.

"Hang on," I yelled as I started to climb the steel support structure.

"Mr. Puffball," said Rosie, training her camera on me. "You'll never make it in time!"

"I catching them!" said Bruiser, dropping the bag and spilling hot dogs, sauerkraut, and little mustard cups everywhere.

Chet, Whiskers, and Kitty ran toward us, trailing a rainbow of melting Italian ices. Whiskers pointed up. "What's Pickles got in his paws?"

I jumped down and squinted at the tiny form. "Bungee cord. I hope that brave little guy knows what he's doing."

If this had been a movie, it would have looked like this:

Pickles ties bungee cord around El Gato and himself

Bruiser prepares to catch them

Pickles lets go

El Gato is saved!

Scrape! The Cyclone started up again, and I saw a car racing right toward Pickles' tiny front paws. Somebody had to do something . . . fast! I ran over to where Bruiser was untangling El Gato. "Bruiser," I yelled, "can you shoot me up there?"

"Yes, I make bungee traption, Mr. Puffyball, but is very danger."

"Danger is my middle name. Let's do it."

Bruiser rigged the bungee cord to a nearby fence like a giant slingshot. And I was the rock ready to be slung. He angled the cord, stretched it back as far as it could go, released, and then *ping!* I flew through the air, straight toward Pickles. I grabbed him, and, through the magic of momentum, just kept going. On and on we flew, over the beach and into the ocean.

As we made our way up the beach, Pickles kept mumbling: "I told you Benedict Cumbercat is a baddie. I told you! I told you!"

"I guess you were right," I said. "So let's make this demo reel the best it can be, get to Hollywood in time, and steal back our movie. Only one more stop."

"Everybody ready?" asked Rosie when we reached the boardwalk.

"But where's El Gato?" I said.

We ran over and spotted El Gato right away. He was slumping toward us with his head down and one paw on his belly. Trailing behind him were my mom and my siblings. Snowball looked angry.

"Looks like we missed some big-time shenanigans," said Chet.

"Mr. Puffball!" shouted my mom. Everybody closed in for a family hug.

"Let me guess," I said. "El Gato ate all the hot dogs and stole your prize."

"He tried," said Snowball. "But he was quickly ejected. The contest was supposed to be between me and the Phantom."

"Hot dogs," said El Gato sadly.

"Actually, he helped me out," Snowball explained. "He ate so many hot dogs before the guards dragged him off, I only had to eat forty-five. That was all that was left, minus the forty-two devoured by the Phantom."

"You mean, you won?"

"And I got the whole thing on film," said my mom. "Even El Gato's bad-boy behavior. I read all about the demo reel in *Variety*." She handed something to Rosie. "Here's footage."

"Thanks," said Rosie, setting up her own camera. "And what have you got to say for yourself, El Gato?"

He looked up with droopy eyes. "I've learned an important lesson today. I can resist hot dogs. I almost did. But there's something I can't resist: the chance to win a trophy."

It was time for me to get into the scene. "So how many hot dogs did you eat, buddy?"

El Gato opened his mouth. I thought he was going to answer. But all he said was, "Sorry."

"For what?"

Then he threw up all over my toes. Which seemed like our cue to leave Brooklyn.

18

Creative Driving

After rinsing my toes off on the Coney Island Board-walk, I said good-bye to my family. "Mom, Snowball, other siblings, it's great to see you. But we've got to get back to Hollywood. You should visit, once our buddy movie comes out."

"As the director," said Rosie, "I've set up El Gato's sleeping bag in the back of the van and surrounded it with buckets. Try and sleep it off, big guy."

"And when we go to Holly-wood," said Bruiser, "I give you new competitions: to fight the flabby by training personal. You become strong, not like bull maybe, but could be like pit bull. Then get Bruiser trophy."

"Great idea!" I said. "But first we show Ms. Bossypaws our impressive demo reel and steal back our buddy movie. We've got three and a half days to go two thousand miles. So let's make like a rocket ship and leave already!"

"Actually, it's 2,814 miles," said Rosie, crinkling her map.

"All those miles? In three days?" said Chet. "You'll never make it!"

"Three and a half. And, by the code of the stunt cats, I will make it."

I quickly drew up a chart to predict the probability of driving 2,814 miles in three and a half days:

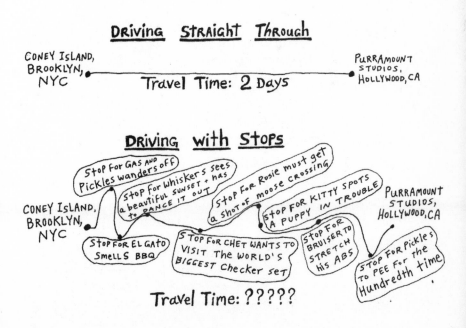

Driving Straight Through

CONEY ISLAND, BROOKLYN, NYC

Travel Time: 2 Days

PURRAMOUNT STUDIOS, HOLLYWOOD, CA

Driving with Stops

CONEY ISLAND, BROOKLYN, NYC

PURRAMOUNT STUDIOS, HOLLYWOOD, CA

Stop for GAS AND Pickles wanders off

Stop for Whiskers sees a beautiful SUNSET + has to DANCE IT OUT

Stop for Rosie must get a shot of moose crossing

Stop for KITTY SPOTS A PUPPY IN TROUBLE

Stop for EL GATO smells BBQ

Stop for CHET WANTS TO VISIT The WORLD'S BIGGEST Checker set

Stop for BRUISER TO STRETCH his ABS

Stop for Pickles To PEE For the Hundredth time

Travel Time: ?????

Next I calculated it as a mathematical equation:

If seven cats and one kitten weighing a total of 89 pounds travel at 60 miles per hour over the course of three and a half days with a wind velocity of 42.6, three tires pumped to 97 percent and the other at 88 percent, over gravelly roads that slow their progress by -2 degrees one-twelfth of the time while reciting poetry from the nineteenth century, how many rocks did Bruiser eat?

Rosie insisted we draw it out as a stop-motion sequence:

Kitty and Chet wrote a song about it, sung while Whiskers danced it out:

Pickles wanted to travel by manga.

Bruiser said it would be faster if he just pushed the van home. And El Gato had this to add:

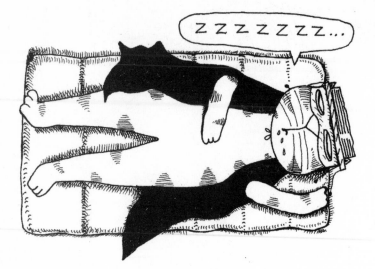

We employed all these tactics and made it to Hollywood in three and a half days by the wet of our noses. All the while Rosie was busy editing our movie on some kind of technological device. She kept muttering things that ranged from "Hmm" to "Too dark" to "Who's that?" to "Looks good to me!"

We drove as far as that dusty hillside overlooking the Valley when I was momentarily distracted by Whiskers saying, "Sweet billboard of Benedict Cumbercat!"

Everybody was okay, but the van was wedged in the "H."

We piled out. El Gato looked at his new watch. "If we're not in the studio in thirty minutes, we're out." He looked at me with sad eyes. "You tried, Mr. Puffball. But I guess this is one contest we're not gonna win."

"Nonsense," I said. "A stunt cat never gives up!" I glanced around desperately. My eyes landed on something that seemed delivered by the fates themselves—a two-cat hang glider. "We're saved! With this tandem glider, we'll be in the studio in five minutes."

El Gato turned a whiter shade of tabby. "No, no, no," he muttered. "El Gato does not fly."

Rosie put a paw on El Gato's shoulder. "How bad do you want that part?"

"Very bad. But I can't fly for real . . ."

"Forget about real! Are you a great actor or aren't you a great actor?"

"I'm a great actor," said El Gato proudly.

"Is there any part too difficult for the great and talented El Gato?"

"Absolutely not."

Rosie set up the camera, popped on a beret, shoved the demo reel into my paws with a wink, and raised her megaphone. "El Gato on set for the big finale! In this scene, you're the brave and fearless Supercat, from the planet Kryptom. Stand here!" Rosie pointed to a spot near the hang glider. "And close your super-hero eyes so your superpower may emerge."

El Gato made an instant transformation. He strode

toward the hang glider with his cape fluttering in the wind, stuck out his chest like a superhero, and closed his eyes. Everybody hurried to strap us into the hang glider.

"Your job, Supercat, is to defeat the nefarious Dr. Woof," continued Rosie. "An angelic soundtrack beckons you on your magnificent quest."

Whiskers and Kitty began to sing, "We are the champions, my feline friend . . ."

"And what's this I hear?" Rosie pointed to Pickles, who mewed like he'd lost his mittens. "An adorable kitten needs saving or the world will devolve into a series of dystopian factions . . ."

I cleared my throat to say, "Wrap it up already!"

"Your superpower is—you can fly!" Rosie continued. "Run, Supercat! Feel the wind beneath your wings!" She gave us a shove, and El Gato and I raced toward the hill's edge. His eyes were still closed. I hoped with every ounce of my body flab this would work. "And now, Supercat, go save that kitten!"

El Gato spread his paws, and we left the ground. And off we sailed into the air, over the Valley, with all of Hollywood laid out below us. We were flying. It was awesome.

I steered us toward Purramount Studios, just like I'd steered myself into the van when running from angry hobos. Just like I steered us all the way from Hollywood to New York and back again.

"Oh, valiant Supercat," I said.

"You're so brave, you can definitely open your eyes!"

The gang and I had killed two proverbial birds with one proverbial stone:

1. Curing El Gato of his fear of flying
2. Getting us to Purramount Studios in time for *Mac & Cheesy's Excellent Adventure* without a second to spare

Or had we?

The British Invasion

It's that excellent part of the movie when the heroes rush in at the last minute to save the day, just like you hoped they would.

Victoria Bossypaws stepped in front of us with her paws crossed over her chest. "What are you two doing here?"

"Sorry, boys," added Director DeMew, "you're not in this movie."

Somebody did that slow clapping that means, *Oh, sure, you deserve applause—not!* and said, with a British accent, "You made it back to Hollywood . . . too late."

I stared into the face of Benedict Cumbercat. Jude Claw stood behind him.

"According to your own grandfather's watch, we're right on time," said El Gato, holding up his wrist.

Benedict smiled like the Grinch who stole Christmas and said, "Oh dear. The watch."

And suddenly everything became crystal clear in one plot-twist-revealing flash. "You deliberately set it to the wrong date, didn't you, Cumbercat? Do you even have a dear departed grandfather?"

"I do," he said. "He is dear, and he departed for England several weeks ago. He's there now, wearing his watch. The one with the correct date. Gentlecats, you've been Cumber-punked."

"You . . . ," I started, shaking my fist in his general direction. But then—

"Yes," said Director DeMew, "we Hollywood types do anything to get ahead. But you went a step too far. Why, Benedict, why?"

Before he could answer, we heard a tinny recording of "God Save the Queen," along with the rumble of eighteenth-century wheels. And then we saw this:

In a moment, the queen was standing before us.

"Your Majesty," said Director DeMew, "we have a saying in America: 'All's fair in love and filmmaking.' With your blessing, we'll all watch El Gato and Mr. Puffball's demo reel and decide who should rightly star in *Mac & Cheesy's Excellent Adventure*."

The queen gave a little royal nod, and off we marched to the Purramount Studios screening room. While somebody set up the demo reel, the rest of the gang arrived.

Miss Bossypaws yelled, "Lights!" And we watched the disaster that was our demo reel.

We all turned to Rosie, who was bright red. "It looked okay in the van."

"Rosie," said Chet gently, "did I ever tell you about my first movie? It totally bombed."

"Thanks for trying to cheer me up, Chet," she said. "But I let everybody down."

"Except the Queen of England," I said, standing and bowing. "Your Majesty, Benedict Cumbercat and Jude Claw are going to make a buddy movie to beat all buddy movies. It will debut in Lon—"

Director DeMew shoved me back into my seat. "I'm the director here! Your Majesty, we're going to make a buddy movie to beat all buddy movies. And it will debut in London!"

Pickles said, "You mean, the baddies won?"

"It's okay, Pickles. We may have lost this battle. But we live on to fight for future roles."

"Actually," said Director DeMew, "I really want El Gato to star in my remake of *Honey, I Shrunk the Kittens* with Meryl Stripe."

He said yes, of course. Nobody turns down a chance to work with Meryl Stripe.

Even though I was happy for El Gato, a sad sigh escaped my lips. Director DeMew spoke up once more. "And Mr. Puffball, we need a stunt cat for Benedict Cumbercat."

Frowny face! If you recall, I vowed in the prologue I would never stunt again forever. But then Director DeMew handed me this:

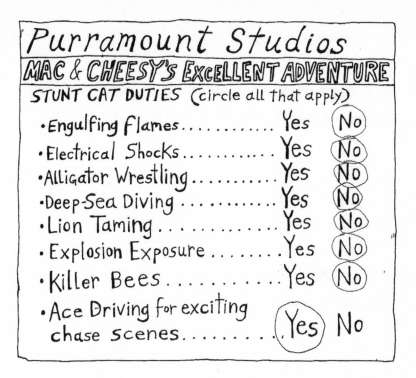

"So all I have to do is be a driving ace?" I said as I looked into Director DeMew's eyes for a long time. "Pinkie swear?"

She held out her pinkie, which is not easy to do when you're a cat, and I stared at it, wondering if I should seal the pinkie deal. Could I really work with *that* cat (even if he had been under orders from Her Majesty the Queen?) Should I go on being a stunt cat, even if it doesn't ignite my inner movie star flames?

I pictured myself driving, dressed like Benedict Cumbercat, yelling things like "Jump over a moving train on my motorbike? Sure, mate!" and "Speed down that mountain like mad? Brilliant!" and "Chase those bobbies? Are you barmy?" All in a British accent.

Maybe I could teach Benedict Cumbercat to treat other actors with respect, even when obeying royals. I'd teach him to be a good uncle to Pickles, who really was a good kitty. And how to say "totally" like a real Californian.

I could do that. But I wanted something more.

"One last thing," I said, seconds before our pinkies intertwined. "I want a speaking part." My eyes darted to Pickles. "And something for my little buddy here."

"Deal," said Director DeMew, patting Pickles' head. "We can always find a part for an adorable kitten. And a talented young cat."

She even gave Pickles a line. With my coaching, he nailed it. And I enjoyed ace driving for the camera. Plus my bit part was pretty sweet. I really got to ham it up.

Epilogue

One Week Later

We were just sitting down to a nice cup of cheese when Whiskers came in and handed us this:

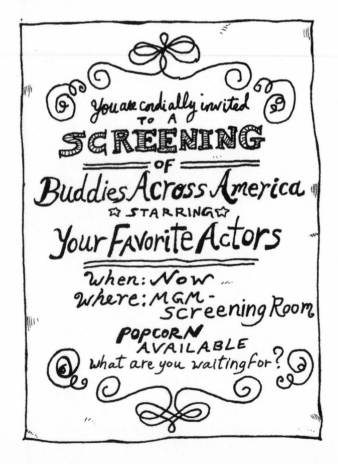

"What's all this about?" I asked.

Kitty stuck her head in and said, "We're ready!"

Chet let out an uncharacteristic giggle. "To the screening room! I'll bring the snacks." He ducked into the kitchen and came out holding bowls of popcorn. "Come on!"

El Gato and I followed him to the screening room. Comfy chairs were set up before the big screen. In the corner stood the potted fern. A red carpet led from the door to the seats.

"Please allow me to escort you two gents," said Kitty. She led us to front-row seats, next to where Pickles was perched on Bruiser's shoulders.

Rosie emerged from the shadows looking absolutely fabulous.

Welcome to the True Meaning of Buddy movie.

Pickles sneezed. Rosie held up her paws for quiet and said, "It was my job to direct and film a demo reel of our wild and crazy adventure across America. I made that demo reel, and it smelled. It smelled bad."

"Like rotten mushrooms in the back of the fridge?" asked Whiskers.

Rosie nodded. "So I made a new movie with a little help from my friends. Whiskers made the sets with cardboard, duct tape, and markers. Kitty made the costumes. Chet thought it should be a silent movie and made dialogue signs. Pickles was Head Prop Cat. Bruiser provided healthy snacks. Everybody chipped in to make this no-budget reenactment of our unforgettable buddy road trip experience. Now grab some popcorn, sit back, and enjoy this exclusive screening."

She nodded to Whiskers, who turned off the lights. Then we all settled in for the best buddy movie ever:

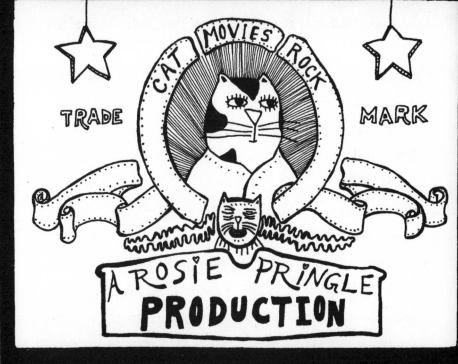

First shot: a classic production logo—Nice!

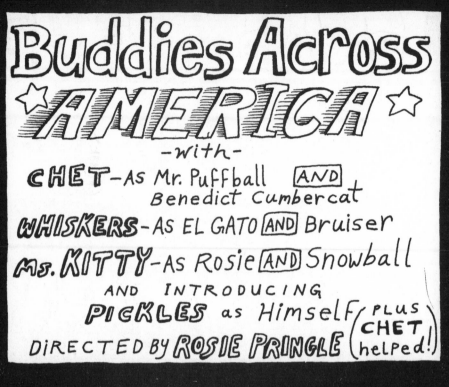

Buddies Across ☆AMERICA☆

-with-

CHET -As Mr. Puffball AND Benedict Cumbercat

WHISKERS -As EL GATO AND Bruiser

Ms. KITTY -As Rosie AND Snowball

AND INTRODUCING

PICKLES as Himself (PLUS CHET helped!)

DiRECTED BY ROSIE PRINGLE

Next—artistically drawn opening credits

Followed by scenes of my
intro to ace driving

And a series re-creating the Cirque du Soleil
Fiasco Fantastico

A fairly realistic sequence of cool cats
leaping the Grand Canyon

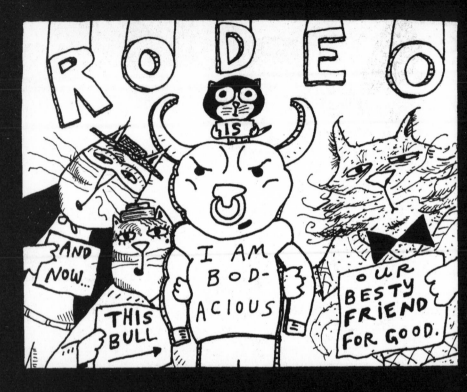

Then the rodeo, ending with this shot—
a true story of unlikely friendship

Through the magic of editing, my role as the Unimportant Sheriff was repurposed.

Reenacted clips of our Coney Island
adventure. Chet looked exactly like
Benedict Cumbercat!

Finally, a bit of truth-stretching to cast us as international heroes. Awesome!

When the movie ended, everybody cheered. The lights went up, and Rosie said, "I still have a lot to learn about being a director."

Chet said, "You're getting there. No need to rush."

"I thought it was great!" I said. "I especially liked the Important Sheriff."

"So do I," said Rosie. "So do I."

SPECIAL FEATURES

INTERACTIVE GAME PAGE

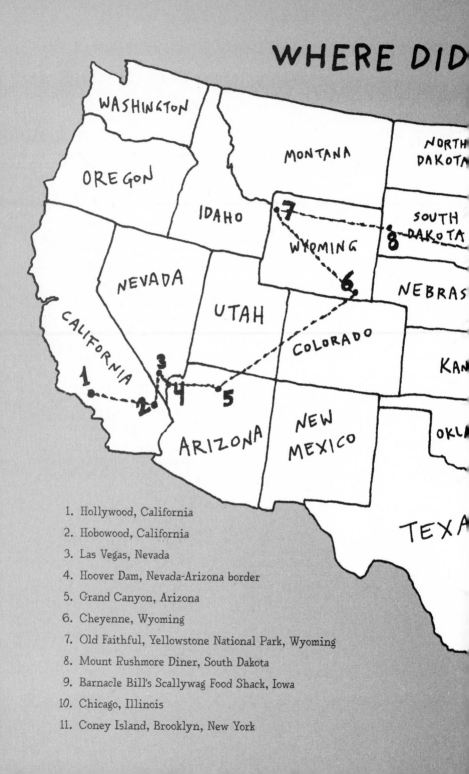

WHERE DID

1. Hollywood, California
2. Hobowood, California
3. Las Vegas, Nevada
4. Hoover Dam, Nevada-Arizona border
5. Grand Canyon, Arizona
6. Cheyenne, Wyoming
7. Old Faithful, Yellowstone National Park, Wyoming
8. Mount Rushmore Diner, South Dakota
9. Barnacle Bill's Scallywag Food Shack, Iowa
10. Chicago, Illinois
11. Coney Island, Brooklyn, New York

THEY GO?

Acknowledgments

Thanks to Leonie Newman for years of encouragement all along my circuitous journey. Thanks to Thomas Newman, who believed in my work since that first picture book. And to Maro Goldstone, who knew I was a cartoonist before I did. Thank you, Jill Davis, for endless patience, guidance, and general sweetness. Lori Nowicki and Claire Easton, I appreciate everything you do, which is a lot! Thanks to the Secret Gardeners for help in every direction and cheerleading, too. To Ro Romanello and Booki Vivat for showing me the value of the collective "meow" and tirelessly promoting Mr. Puffball. You guys are the best! Many thanks to Katie Fitch and Amy Ryan for design magic extraordinaire. And of course to Alana Whitman for getting Mr. Puffball on TV! Thanks to designer Carla Weise and to everybody at HarperCollins from copyediting and design to marketing, publicity, and sales . . . you're all superstars in my book! Continued appreciation to Katherine Tegen and now Nancy Inteli for turning my dream into a reality. Thank you, Alan Gratz and Megan Shepherd and all the NC kid-lit community, for navigational assistance at every turn! Thank you, SCBWI, for helping me become a "success story." Thanks to my adorable friend Linda Marie Barrett and to Malaprop's Bookstore for an unforgettable launch party and enthusiastic support for me and all local authors. Thank you, Donna McCalman, for welcoming Mr. P to Tennessee. Appreciation for everybody in my extended family and universe of friends who came out big-time for Mr. Puffball. Thank you, Sal, for my first fan letter. Big heart-filled hugs and kisses for my husband, Hank Bones, wordsmith genius like no other, driving ace, and easy on the eyes to boot. A world of gratitude for my daughter, Madeline, for smiles, laughs, hugs, and trying to teach me how to draw manga. (I almost got it!)

CONSTANCE LOMBARDO

is living the dream. And not the one where she's back in high school and can't remember her locker combination. There are at least four happy things in her life currently:

1. She has two books about cats in her local bookstore and other locales as well as two actual, fluffy cats. One of them is probably napping with her right now.

2. She has gotten e- and snail mail from actual kids from North Carolina to California. Some even had drawings!

3. She may travel from North Carolina to California with her friend Cynthia. The concept: a cross-country road trip so they could eat right across America and see the world's biggest ball of twine. C'mon, Cynthia!

4. Some of her friends like to play Pictionary.

DID YOU KNOW . . . (fun facts about the author)

- Like Mr. Puffball, she learned how to drive later than most. Though not exactly an "ace driver," she has been known to hang an impressive left turn.

- In her opinion, cats should not drive on the highway. They should probably stay in the bike lane since their cars are so small.

- She has never been to the Grand Canyon, Las Vegas, the Hoover Dam, or Mount Rushmore. She did go to Wisconsin once and found it right above Illinois.

- Constance once had a kitten named The Phantom.

- Ms. Lombardo has not had one cookie today. (unverified)